# THE SACRED BAND TRINITY

## PART 1

✦ ✦ ✦

## PALLADIUM

James MacTavish

## Red Dragon
Sir Galahad
(Richard Allen)
Sir Gawain
(William Wood)
Sir Bors
(Nick Butcher)
Sir Kay
(Karen Milligan)
Sir Gaheris
(Gary Willis)
Sir Bedivere
(Mack Benson)

## White Dragon
Sir Lancelot
(Sir Lawrence Worthington)
Sir Tristan
(Tristan Baker)
Sir Geraint
(Geraint South)
Sir Gareth
(Colonel Stephen Thorpe)
Sir Palamedes
(Mohammed Hussin)
Sir Lamorak
(Michael Von Lamorak...dec. WW2)

## The Battle of Chaeronea
## 338 BC

'Upon whom now shall we bestow the title "Lord of all Greece?"' came the solemn words of Chares, casting a steady but forlorn gaze across a sea of thirty thousand Macedonian spears. There was a time not so long ago when the aged Athenian general would have welcomed a horizon teeming with the banners of his rival northern kin as the hot-blooded thirst for war took hold like a venom, spurring even the most fragile of infantry to grasp the hilt and slash and stab in a frenzy, drunk on rage, adrenaline and passion.

Lysicles tugged gently at the reins of his horse, contemplating his response. 'Was there ever a chance? A challenge? A rebuke from Athens or Zeus himself against King Phillip?' eventually came the rhetorical salvo, laced with both fear and anger. 'The moment that obsequious snake Philippides paid homage to this Macedonian swine I felt the beating heart of Greek warriors. Decades of war, for some families three generations of men taking up arms to defend their lands from Greeks and Persians alike, let down by silk-clad, gluttonous bureaucrats, sitting in their palatial abodes, all too willing to kneel before those who will promise them a steady stream of wine!'

Chares snapped from his despondency for a brief moment and pointed.

'I hear Phillip has risked the life of his own 18-year-old son in this battle? There, on the left flank.'

'Yes, Alexander. Quite the strategist some say. Destined for greatness, say others,' Lysicles retorted.

'Perhaps deservedly so – to engage the left-flank is to engage the formidable. Sons of Ares. The Lions of Leuctra.' Chares continued with a glimmer of hope that maybe this torn battlefield might yet yield a trophy scalp.

'Perhaps. I care not for Thebean blood or the so-called legends that flow within,' came Lysicles' crass reply. 'Still … if given the choice …'

✢   ✢   ✢

Archelaus held his shield high, absorbing the blows of bronze blades crashing down upon it. His knees buckled at the second hit, sending him to the ground. 'Where is he?' Has he fallen?' Knowing the third hit would undoubtedly break not only his shield but his spirit, the relief of meeting Charon on the shores of the River Styx began to seep into his veins. This calm was split by a flash of blue light glimpsed in the corner of his eye, quickly followed by the weak last cries of several Macedonian soldiers.

The outstretched arm of Damon greeted Archelaus, hauling him to his feet. 'What kept you?' Archelaus softly mocked as they embraced.

'I can't watch you all the time ...' Damon managed to stutter out before slanting heavily to one side, clutching his side.

'You're injured.' Archelaus fussed, placing his hand over Damon's wound, trying to stop the blood now welling between his fingers.

'Can you stand?'

'Do I have a choice? Look at us. We're overrun!'

'How many of the Band are left?'

'Hard to say. I saw Dwight and Egor both fall. Dinis and Dimitri fell back to the Well with whoever was left. A last stand.'

Archelaus lifted and steadied Damon over his broad shoulders 'Fall back. Band of Thebes, *fall back*.' he bellowed with all he could muster. Damon winced as Archelaus twisted his body in a frantic series of swipes and thrusts from his sword, cutting down adversaries in their path of retreat. A careless deflection of an opposing blade split his weapon, but the broken tip was all that was needed to pierce the throat, setting off a quick spray of blood across both their faces.

Breathing heavily on his neck, 'You never were the best when it came to a blade.' Damon wheezed, '... so clumsy!'

Archelaus managed to crack a quick smile before refocusing. 'Some cover please? Give me a chance to have you retreat in one piece.'

Upon hearing Archelaus' command, Damon gripped his companion's upper arm tightly and raised his own fist in salute. A shimmering blue band circled his wrist just at the moment two Macedonians launched a direct frontal assault, both their spears in full charge, only to splinter within inches of Damon's forearm. Their momentary perplexity was enough for Archelaus to summon a flash of blue flame and hurl it, melting both bodies.

'We can't keep on like this' Damon confessed in a weakening tone.

'We can! We're not far from the Well … and support. I hope.'

'Phillip will get what he came for. We have failed. The Band has …'

Damon's apparent capitulation was interrupted by the chant of the famed Theban war cry. 'We are the *Lions*. We are the *Lions*.' A rallying shiver went down their spines, as they heard the voices of brothers in harmony echoing back to the great general Pelopidas and join with the shower of sparks of blue flame across the cindered sky, deep into the Macedonian phalanx, despite knowing its meaning and inevitable outcome.

'We should get to the Well now!' Archelaus commanded.

'We can't leave the Band!' spat Damon, fingers fumbling wearily over his short scabbard. 'We m-must … stand …!' he muttered, panting.

'Well. *Now.*' snapped Archelaus.

Their feet slid through the mud of the battlefield, the cries of their brothers slowly fading. A few isolated spears and abandoned shields bearing the double-headed dragon insignia of Cadmus protruding out of the ground entranced Damon as he slipped in and out of consciousness. Youthful memories were evoked, the stories of old – uttered around crackling campfires to aspiring young men and women of Thebes.

✦   ✦   ✦

'Cadmus is Father to us all' dictated one scholar. 'Slayer of the fabled Dragon of Ares sent as punishment for drinking from his sacred well'. The youngest in the audience would always give an audible gasp upon mention of the word *Dragon*. 'An act that would have seen the unleashing of the full wrath of our God of War had it not been for our fair Maiden of Wisdom Athena and her cunning intervention.' Gasps would turn to reverent smiles and nods of approval once the Daughter of Zeus made her appearance.

"Sow the Dragon's teeth!" She would say,' continued the scholar, 'Let the spirits of the Spartoi, undead warriors of fury, descend upon you and prove your valour to my brother.' The teeth were sown deep into the earth, and from them sprang forth the armed animated corpses ... putrefying facial flesh exposing full teeth and mandibles, bare-boned fingers rattling against rusted spears with a hiss of malice coming from behind dented and scratched shields.

'How can one man defeat such an army? An army of the undead?' Cadmus would cry. This is when Athena meekly presented to him a jewel, a ruby of deepest crimson, and placed it firmly in our hero's hand. Nothing more was said, and our Maiden disappeared back to the heights of Mount

Olympus, leaving a fear-stricken Cadmus opposing the dreaded Spartoi.

The jewel was heavy for such a small token, no power or magic visible as Cadmus attempted to control the shaking of his hand to inspect it. All that could be noticed was its incandescence, which caught the lifeless eyes of the Spartoi, even to the point where weapons were lowered, crumbling chest armour fully exposed, mesmerised. Resisting the temptation to plunge his own sword into the nearest vulnerable foe, Cadmus quickly calculated that little could kill what is already dead … save the dead themselves? Without hesitation, he threw the object of their apparent desire casually over his shoulder, an act swiftly followed by a collective howl of lust from Spartoi warriors. Rushing past him in blatant disregard, the live corpses threw themselves at the jewel, mindlessly scrabbling at first, then becoming more resentful of each other as greed took hold.

'Limbs were severed. Spines crushed!' theatrically gestured the scholar, his enthusiasm for such a grisly tale starting to unnerve some of the mothers and fathers in the audience. 'All consumed by the most uncontrollable aspect of the human psyche – *desire*. Our Founder needed but watch, as his enemy ripped itself apart until none stood.' Children's eyes, wide with wonder, mused over the cautionary tale of their evening's entertainment.

'Did Cadmus get to keep the jewel then?' called out a curious girl from the front row.

'Ah yes, yes he did,' the scholar responded, resuming his seat after regaling them with such drama. 'But not before our

Maiden of Wisdom returned with a gift far greater, one born from the love and the pain experienced by Athena herself ...'

'Was it a sword?' cried a boy, eagerly interrupting. '*No. A spear?*' shouted another, as smiles and laughs began to break from the adult members of the audience.

'Neither,' the scholar confirmed. 'It was but a small statue, feminine in shape, no more than a hoplite's foot high'.

'A statue?' mocked the same girl who had inquired about the fate of the jewel. 'I would have kept the jewel!' she proclaimed, triggering a playful rolling of eyes from her parents.

'And such is the nature of us mortals,' the scholar intoned heavily. 'We see only the prize, not the beauty, and alas, poor Cadmus proved no different'.

'But he was a *hero*. No Greek could ever match him in battle! He was like Perseus, Hercules, Bellafer...Bellapher....Ber....Ber...' a boy tripped over his tongue trying to recall his trio of heroes.

'Bellerophon,' the scholar completed. 'And you are quite right, young master. Cadmus was indeed a hero. He was strong, quick, skilled with both spear and shield, and had the honour of drinking from the Well of Ares, upon which our very State is founded. But ... all heroes have their weaknesses, don't they?' came the rhetorical response. 'For all the strength that came from this Well that runs deep beneath our feet, we mortals always crave for more'.

Cadmus had created the envy of all of Greece in Thebes. Strength, wisdom and power through its people, enough to keep all its rivals in effective servitude. Cadmus, of course, could take his pick of the loveliest of companions, and when that time came, the young Lord of Greece didn't settle for any woman that stood before him, but rather, one that was looking down upon him. In an act of defiance to his own deities, he importuned Athena for the hand of the daughter of Ares, the ethereal Harmonia. Knowing her vengeful brother would never allow such a union, Athena prepared herself to become the bearer of bad news to her beloved champion, when a surprising turn of events unfolded before her. Ares, perhaps flattered by this mortal's beguilement, agreed to Cadmus's demands. Harmonia was presented to Cadmus as his faithful wife, a gift to the greatest race in all the land, and blessed their marriage with the very jewel that won Cadmus his glory, set in a necklace adorning his cherished daughter, worn during the nuptials and forever henceforth.

'But our Gods are endlessly playing games with us,' warned the scholar, leaning forward and wagging his finger in warning. 'For what appears as appeasement is rarely done without an ulterior motive. Yes, Harmonia was beautiful, but goddesses never age and can grow to be the envy of us mere mortals. The Lady of Thebes saw her once-great husband tire and weep like the first flowers of spring as the years flowed by. She found comfort in other suitors, younger men who now threatened Cadmus' very throne. Our Founder could no longer contain his grief at not matching his spouse's lust and youthfulness, and eventually, both his will and his heart caved in, as many an old man does, to power-hungry stallions so eager to take his place. He cursed the day he dared impose his demands upon the gods and passed across the River Styx a spiteful and saddened man.'

'So, our great hero died upset because of a woman?' guffawed one of the boys, before turning to his friend who sat next to him. 'Told you. Girls are nothing but trouble!' the two giggled, only to be given a clip around the ear by both their mothers, who sat directly behind them.

'Sir...?' came the meek voice of a girl with her hand up, addressing the scholar. 'What about the Sacred Band? My Uncle Alessandro has just been called up as a fighter, just last month ... surely they wouldn't have fallen when Harmonia arrived?'

The scholar sat back and turned to look through the small arched window by his side, framing the Temple of Eros that sat high in the Catherian Mountains overlooking the Citadel of Cadmea. 'Your uncle brings your family great honour for earning such a selection, for the Band is said to represent all that is pure in Thebes – love, loyalty, sacrifice and strength. But no matter what their virtues, their service is to the king of our land, whoever may be sitting on the throne. That is both their blessing and their curse'.

✦        ✦        ✦

'Damon ... *Damon*.' called Archelaus, waking him from his reverie. 'We're almost back at the citadel. We can get to the temple before the Macedonians and ...'

'We're *cursed* Archelaus.' Damon deliriously blurted, pushing his heavily built companion away to arm's length. 'Thebes.

Cadmus. Ares. This is what becomes of us. It was foretold! We Greeks … always wanting more, grasping at what cannot be touched, trying to control what cannot be controlled ….' His words faded as his breath drained out of him, only to fall back into the arms of Archelaus.

Setting Damon down to his knees in an attempt to ease his suffering and sorrow, Archelaus pressed his forehead to his and placed a comforting hand under the side of his jaw. 'We made an oath; we swore to Athena herself, remember? We stand, until struck down by spear or blade or … a lightning bolt from Zeus himself.' Archelaus said with a slight chuckle upon hearing his own words. Brushing Damon's dark, matted curls of hair out of his eyes and fixing him with his gaze – 'We're not forsaking that oath now. I am not abandoning you. You understand?' As they embraced tightly, through fresh tears Damon saw over his partner's shoulder the Temple of Eros, bringing a moment of clarity and relief as he recalled everything the two of them had achieved together. Archelaus opened his eyes to meet the standards of Macedonian soldiers slowly marching towards them, helmets casting shade across all but their parched lips and stubble.

A solitary figure appeared through the haze on horseback, looking majestic against an orange sky. His stature was difficult to determine, but his blond hair was long, and his complexion still beardless. A gesture of his hand brought his mercenaries to a standstill, his steed tossing his head restlessly, only to be calmed by 'Steady, Bucephalus.'

Archelaus' mind clicked over in a frenzy while still holding Damon tightly. The mounted figure cocked his head to one side while inspecting the two soldiers in front of him, all the time caressing in small circles a small red gem on display over his tunic. Archelaus' eyes grew narrower, his teeth grinding, summoning his strength to his left hand in a blue flame ready to strike. But the chance was never granted.

The mounted figure dropped from his horse and removed his helmet as he walked through his own men towards the two bodies lying blood-soaked, but hands still gripping each other where they fell. A respectful nod was all he could allow himself in front of his victorious subjects, despite aching to offer more. He then cast his glare upon the Citadel of Cadmea, and the Temple of Eros beyond.

**Chapter 2**
Al-Khums, Libya
20th May 2011 AD

Adam had travelled to North Africa twice before, and on both occasions confessed to being disappointed. Despite a passion for history, the family holiday to Tunis when he was eight years old denied him a trip to Carthage in favour of a tired package-deal hotel complete with a chipped-tiled, scummy swimming pool and enough sun-crisped tourist skin to last a lifetime. A college school trip the second time around held high hopes, with an itinerary that included the fabled Pyramids of Giza, Karnack and the Valley of the Kings – only to be greeted by the dense smog of Cairo and the glow of the fast-food golden arches actually casting some light over Cheops' last remaining Wonder of the World.

Dusk was settling in on this cool spring evening, with Adam growing increasingly uncomfortable, having lain on the hot sand for nearly four hours, sheltered by a few isolated desert palms and only the sea breeze for company. He'd been observing the crumbling ruins of Leptis Magna intermittently for several days now, watching trucks moving to and from the site, disappearing behind the high canvasses that enveloped the Basilica of Septimus Severus.

While there was a time when many would come and visit this well-preserved site honoured by the Roman Emperor nearly two thousand years ago, it was now strictly off-limits. One need only hold their ears to the ground and listen to the occasional tremble of missiles and machine gun fire evidencing the bitter civil war that had consumed the country since February. Not one for modern journalism, Adam had picked his way through several articles, from the BBC to Al-Jazeera, to try and form an unbiased view of the situation, although he just found himself lamenting the loss of so many significant historical sites each time such conflicts escalated from here right across the northern Sahara into the Middle East.

'This is not for my own academic pleasure. This is not for me,' he would play over and over in his head, reciting the same words given to him by his father just before departure. She *needs* help. Something has gone wrong. The moon's first light had just bathed the site when an atypical vehicle arrived— polished, pedestrian, as if it had not seen anything but tarmac before now. It was heavily guarded on both flanks by two more suitable vehicles from which armed soldiers appeared, immediately conducting a brief survey. Out of the protected car came a well-presented figure, hard to make out with the naked eye, but met promptly by a decorated militant with a warm handshake, then escorted behind the canvas. Adam reached for his binoculars, fiddling with the focus, trying to determine the approximate number of armed guards and the means of entry before choosing his cue. A single flare in his right pocket was drawn while he rose to his feet, the cap clicked off, erupting in sparks of brilliant white before being dropped by his side.

The response was immediate – guards shouted in Arabic and began to move in unison towards the decoy as Adam scrambled down the bank as inconspicuously as he could, rolling quickly to the side of canvas. A momentary hesitation as muffled voices from within the tent tried to assess the commotion outside. A chance to slip underneath and head straight for the cover of the solid wooden desk pressed up against one of the broken, ruined columns.

Adam caught his breath and rolled his broad shoulders to help shake off his tumble into the tent. He listened carefully to whatever ongoing conversation was still taking place among those within, thankfully and not entirely to his surprise, now mostly in English.

'And these carvings say what exactly?' the well-dressed gentleman enquired, leaning in between the desk and the column to inspect them, letting Adam assess him better – pressed suit, trimmed beard and native complexion, walking with a small wooden staff no higher than his breast.

'Well, as our resident expert, Mr Hussin, we were hoping you could tell us. And why exactly have you asked for this site to be ring-fenced by my men?' the decorated military man replied. He went on to ramble off-topic about the significance of the National Liberation Army and the movement of the people in defiance of the corrupt dictatorship that had poisoned Libya, a rambling that appeared completely inconsequential to Mr Hussin.

'The woman?' interjected Mr Hussin. 'You said you'd apprehended a woman?'

'The English girl?' the militant snapped back. 'She was found at this site by my men a week ago. Claimed she was a British tourist, but not many regular tourists take out four of my men armed only with a *stick.*' he continued with a hint of embarrassment. Adam smiled inside upon hearing this account—sounds like Karen to me.—he thought.

'Where is she now?' asked Mr Hussin.

'Out the back there' the militant pointed. 'While we were sceptical of her confession, she is a British national, and the last thing our movement wanted was the perceived abuse of a citizen of one of our international allies, so we kept her here as instructed.' The conversation trailed off as the two moved to the rear of the tent. Adam gingerly lifted his head from hiding and scouted around before creeping towards the ornate carvings.

Starring up at the nearly five-metre-high column, he could not help but be impressed by its precision and craftsmanship – this was a labour of love. Adam crouched down to inspect its base and saw the carving of the feminine, regal hand stretched high as if supporting its masculine counterparts that followed above. She was the cornerstone, the beginning, the key. The worn carvings were hard for Adam to interpret, but it appeared as though this female hand held aloft something small, a sword maybe? A stone? No, too well carved for either of those. Another statue? Adam continued to ponder as the noises from outside grew louder, breaking his concentration and instinctively drawing his hand down towards the holster on his hip. Time to go.

'Karen. What did you find here?' he whispered to himself in pursuit of Mr Hussin and his apparent ally. Of equal significance was Mr Hussin himself – what was an educated local doing out here during such a crisis? Hardly the time for excavation pleasures. Maybe not, he thought again, recalling his own heartbreak at treasured history being wiped out on the whim of societal upheaval. Perhaps this was a bold attempt to salvage whatever the Libyan people could before the fires of war took everything? Mr Hussin the champion benefactor of UNESCO or something.

Taking cover again behind a fragile stone wall, Adam stood calmly and listened to the revived conversation between Mr Hussin and the general, who now had a name, General Salem. In a shard of mirror Adam could see Karen, head hung low, tied in a chair and illuminated by a spotlight. Mr Hussin and the general were casting imposing shadows over her.

'She's not spoken these last few days, apart from expressing her demands to return to the British Embassy' snorted the general.

Mr Hussin approached cautiously, before using the end of his staff to tilt Karen's weeping head up, her blue eyes like daggers. 'Not the most appropriate time to be vacationing in Libya my dear.' Mr Hussin addressed her softly. 'Might one ask why you came to Al-Khums? To this very site?'

Karen appeared transfixed for a few moments before nonchalantly blowing one of her rich brown strands of hair out of her face. 'Well, you know. Thought I'd give this place a final look before you idiots blow it to hell!' she sparked, darting a glaze towards the general in disgust. The general sneered his disapproval while Mr Hussin gave a modest chuckle.

'You must care passionately about your history, Mrs …?'

'Wood.'

'Mrs Wood. And why, might I ask, *this* particular site?'

'What? Do you want me to give you a history lesson? Roman? Byzantine? What would you like? Why does everything need a reason for you trigger-happy types?'

'Because there is a war on, Mrs Wood. A dangerous civil war. Hardly safe for a *tourist*?' Mr Hussin cast quizzically.

'No kidding! I read the brochure.' Karen blasted back.

General Salem was looking increasingly tense. 'This is no *tourist*.' he erupted while marching over to within a breath of Adam's position and the small chest on the other side of the wall.

'Look at what we found in her satchel. A notebook with the times of daily arrival and departure of your own personnel, Mr Hussin. Photographs of the site at different times of the day. The phone is locked but we can tell it has been used to call foreign numbers! This is no tourist...this is a *journalist*. Or worse still, a *spy*.' shouted the general. 'And as for her wielding of *this* ...' he held up the metre-long wooden stick, 'a highly trained one at that.'

Mr Hussin tried to settle the atmosphere, leaning against his own staff with exasperation. 'Look, Mrs Wood, I'm sure you'll agree this does not add up. Now, the general and I are very busy men and we would appreciate it if you just came clean and confessed your true purpose here. As you are a UK citizen, I can guarantee your safety.'

Karen pondered Mr Hussin's proposal for a second, then took another look at Mr Hussin, her glare drifting just to his side, then snapping back in silent rebuke.

Mr Hussin sighed. 'My apologies, General Salem. We appear to be wasting our time here. Might I suggest you continue to show me the rest of this site and I will speak with my own men here in the morning. I'm keen to hear what they have to say about their encounter with Mrs Wood.'

The general nodded his agreement and escorted Mr Hussin away, but not before Karen slipped in the final word. 'How long have you had trouble walking, Mr Hussin?' she softly asked. Mr Hussin paused for an uncomfortable moment, only to click his neck and continue to walk away.

Adam seized his chance, quickly filling the vacated space. 'Karen? Karen?'

She took a second or two to refocus. 'Adam! What on earth? Richard sent you?'

Not sure whether to be flattered or insulted, Adam cut away the chair's restraints while Karen continued to fluster.

'Were you seen?'

'Thanks – real confidence boost that.'

'Sorry...not at my best.'

'Neither will I be if we don't leave now.' Adam waited impatiently as Karen scooped up her evidence and tucked the stick under her arm.

'Which way?' Adam demanded.

'There's a secondary road, unlit … they use it sometimes to evade …' She got no further before a mercenary's bellow echoed through the tent. Adam's diversionary flare now burnt out. The commotion saw armed silhouettes cast outside the canvas, rallying before pouring through the tent's main entrance.

Neither Adam nor Karen were overly fluent in Libyan, but no translation was needed as assault rifles were pointed squarely at their torsos. Both instinctively ignored the command not to move. Adam without hesitation pulled out his pistol and fired at the lamp hanging to one side, sending a splash of sparks over the ringleader as Karen threw the chair as hard as she could, clocking one hard on the head. The response was immediate but uncoordinated, punching holes into the canvas as they fled.

'Take a right. Right!' Karen barked, with Adam in tow. A winding stone corridor opened into the excavated marketplace, loose flagstones underfoot causing both to trip.

'Which way now?' Adam continued, frantically turning his head to look behind.

'Keep going straight. Head to the Amphitheatre, we can lose them there.'

A few stray bullets struck the surrounding ancient masonry as the two bolted for the cover of more rock slabs. Karen could hear more voices directly in front of them and rapidly tried to rethink her strategy as Adam remained fixed on their pursuers, sending the occasional shot their way.

'Running out of options here.' he remarked as impassively as he could.

Karen twisted her head round in every direction before selecting an option. 'Quick...down that tunnel. It leads under the Amphitheatre.' she beckoned.

Karen rolled down as Adam ran and slid close behind, checking his remaining ammo. The tunnel was narrow, Adam's broad shoulders just squeezing through as Karen continued to navigate. 'Not far … just up here! There's a little artificial light, thank God.'

'*Ouch*.' Adam winced as he hit his head on a low wooden beam.

'Yeah – watch out for those.' Karen chuckled as she asked Adam to give her a boost up through a small hole in the theatre floor. '*Come on*.' as her hand stretched down to help pull Adam through.

Karen wasn't wrong about the lack of light. The vast amphitheatre cocooned them, amplifying the sounds of the sea wind rustling in the shrubs. But it was still quiet, too quiet for Adam's liking.

'Where to now?' he whispered.

'The secondary road is just over the other side. I take it Richard didn't plan a welcome party?'

'You know my dad. Fend for yourself and all that.'

'Typical.'

They continued forward with whispers and trepidation, Karen beginning to relax a little as the coast drew near. 'There's sometimes the odd truck on the secondary road, rarely guarded. If we can …'

'Wait.' Adam cut off.

'What?'

What was once friendly darkness was pierced by four spotlights fiercely zoning in upon them, accompanied by the urgent barking of commands and clicking of rifles. The seating area of the ancient theatre accommodated several armed guards in desert military attire, with Mr Hussin standing full centre next to General Salem.

'Mrs Wood. You didn't say you were expecting company?' Mr Hussin mocked, still leaning on his staff.

Adam and Karen stood fast. Adam's gun was raised, pointing in their direction. Neither could muster any worthy response.

'Well, what a shame. I was getting the sense we could have learned a lot from one another, an awful lot.' He continued. 'Alas, you're starting to make me re-evaluate my offer of sanctuary.' Rubbing his hand over his cheek absentmindedly, General Salem turned to his men and gave an authoritative nod as their rifles were raised.

Karen's hand shuddered as she brushed it against Adam's and the two exchanged an intimate glance. The general's order was given and a volley of bullets followed, some missing their target and causing sand to puff up, obscuring the view. The firing stopped in satisfaction, only to be met with disappointment.

A faint blue ring of light encircled Adam, Karen safely behind him, shielded. Adam had his fist in front of his chest, slightly bowed at the knees, eyes clenched shut, then they flicked open while he exhaled in relief.

General Salem turned to Mr Hussin in astonishment. Mr Hussin appearing completely unfazed. 'You were right, General Salem. No *tourist*.'

Before any new order was given, Karen held her stick high and let out a deep cry before plunging it into the ground, casting a radiant white light which blinded all before it.

'Go ... *Go!*' Karen yelled in Adam's ear, as her conjured light faded. They sprinted to the far side of the theatre and up over the steps two at a time. Panicked shouts came from behind them as General Salem and his men rushed to reorganise. Adam knew they did not have long.

'How far?' he wheezed.

'Just ahead. *Look.*' Karen gestured excitedly with her stick towards two battered old trucks on a freshly worn coastal path. 'We can get down the side on the wooden scaffold.'

The two jumped from plank to worn plank, struggling to balance. Karen proved the nimbler of the two, reaching the ground first. '*Quickly.*' she shouted back at Adam, only to see one of the planks give way under his feet, forcing him to leap for the beam above. 'Christ. Watch out!' she yelled.

'Thanks.' Adam caustically responded as he swung athletically from beam to farthest foothold, only to be met with a firm kick to the midriff from Mr Hussin.

'*Adam*' Karen screamed.

'Go. *Get out of here.*' Adam snapped as he got to feet. The gaunt but imposing frame of Mr Hussin towered over him, removing his pressed suit jacket and rolling up his sleeves with unsettling confidence.

'I'm sorry Sir, I don't believe we've been properly introduced?' came that same calm but commanding tone.

Adam wasted no time engaging. No pistol on either side, but Mr Hussin proved remarkable nimble with his staff. Every punch thrown was swiftly blocked, every kick evaded. He was trained – a fair match to Adam. A firm thrust of his staff into Adam's gut winded him and forced him to the edge of the scaffolding plank. Fingertips hooked on the frame edge to remain upright, Adam took advantage of an over-enthusiastic lunge by Mr Hussin, twisting and switching places with him to land a hard kick to the back of his knee, bringing his opponent down.

Thinking he had the upper hand, Adam went to kick again but Mr Hussin saw it coming and blocked with his staff. The countermove was enough to clip Adam sharply on a defensive forearm ... the blow curiously not registering as a blunt object should. Staggering back, with Mr Hussin returning to his feet, Adam raised his fist once more, bringing the safety of the blue circle, shimmering intermittently as he focused. The staff of his opponent again came down, this time with much more force, a surprising force. Adam's eyes were tight when he hit the deck once again, shaking his head to regain composure just in time to see Mr Hussin preparing to strike once more – this time no chance of staging any defence of any kind ... then came a crash from directly below.

Karen had been busy with one of the abandoned vehicles, ploughing full throttle into the foundations of the wooden scaffold. Planks toppled down in clouds of dust, with Adam and Mr Hussin falling either side of the truck. Karen flung the side door open – 'Get in!' Adam hauled himself onto the passenger seat just as she locked the shift in reverse, tyres spinning uselessly on the loose sand before finally gaining a grip. With a competent hand behind the wheel, the truck spun 180 degrees and pounced forward with a roar of the engine.

'You OK?' she asked seconds later.

'Yeah. Still watching Top Gear I see.' Adam tried to joke while nursing his forearm.

'Well, I'm 46 years old and live in Bath. What else is there to do on a Sunday?' came Karen's chirpy response. 'Is anyone following us?'

'No, I don't think so.'

'Your arm, is it broken?'

Adam inspected it. 'No, I don't think so'. Karen took her eyes briefly off the road to assess for herself.

'What did that man hit you with? A blade?' she questioned.

'That staff of his. But something…. something unusual about it I'd say. Not sure'. Adam muttered, replaying the confrontation in his head.

'A staff that not only broke your shield, but also cut you? I'd agree about *unusual*.' she concurred, full of concern.

'Cut me?' Adam interjected as he took a closer look at his supporting hand, now smeared bright red. He was bleeding.

**Chapter 3**
**Boston, USA**
**4th July 2011 AD**

*'As God was with our Fathers, so may He be with Us'.* Luke reflected deeply on this; the motto of the city he had called home for the past eight years since crossing the Atlantic in haste. 'Fathers? Be with us?' he scoffed as he peered through the dusty blinds that kept the morning sun out of his small bedroom, in a modest apartment within sight of Massachusetts State House. Today was a double anniversary, being the birthday both of the United States, and of his mother, fast asleep in the room next door.

Rising from his bed with a stretch, and blinking in the full summer sunshine as he raised the blinds, he stumbled over to the pile of clothes heaped in a corner, giving each garment a quick shake before dressing. Despite the occasion, Luke had never been one for formality, and having spent most of his teenage years in England, not really accustomed to bathing himself in the Red, White and Blue each Independence Day – but for his mother, he'd at least splash on a little aftershave.

Mornings had become a tiresome routine of late, labouring down the creaking staircase to the kitchen-cum-lounge area, kettle on for coffee, see what juice was left in the fridge and usually tossing a few pop tarts into the toaster. Skipping through whatever mail lay on the floor by the door, Luke would always conduct a scan and count the number of empty wine bottles left on the small glass table by the patched two-seater sofa ... only three today.

Distraction came from the light buzz of his mobile in his pocket – 'Hey Babe. Yes, happy Fourth of July to you too ... no, I haven't forgotten, I'll pick you up in thirty minutes,' he said, trying to pour hot water into two mugs while looking at his watch. Dashing back upstairs, he gave a loud knock on his mother's bedroom door. 'Mom? You up?' was met with a low groan inside. Luke pushed the door open gently and tiptoed in, placing one mug by the bedside. His mother breathed deeply, disturbed by the intrusion, but nodded her approval upon the smell of Nescafé.

'What time is it, Love?' she grumbled, rubbing the sleep from her eyes.

'9 a.m. And you're forty years plus nine.' he chuckled mildly.

'Thanks for the reminder ... might as well round it up, hadn't we?' she joked while taking a sip. 'Plans for today, Love?'

'It's Saturday. Minnie just called – picking her up from the pool then we'll likely go down to the harbour front, check out what time the fireworks are tonight, grab some lunch probably.'

His mother sighed remembering the date and no doubt the full day of disturbances from the neighbourhood. 'Well ... I watch them from the window.' she responded dismissively.

'Did you want to come with us? Just for this evening? Might do you good?'

'No thanks Love, honestly. Might call Cathy from over the road later, think we're at least a season behind now on True Blood,' taking another satisfying sip.

'Fair enough.' Luke said stepping away. 'Might not be back until late, just so you know.'

'How does Mary do it?' she muttered within earshot. 'History degree, competitive swimming, out late with friends….'

'Putting up with me, don't forget!' Luke grinned warmly, interrupting.

'That too.' she smiled. 'Have fun, Sweetheart.'

Although comfortable with the teasing every so often from family and friends, Luke did sometimes wonder whether he and Mary were destined to last. They certainly shared the same humour, wit and apparent social sparks – one of Mary's friends often describing her quaintly as 'the life of the party.' While Luke was no wallflower, keeping company with a group of Harvard post-grads while having to admit he was a lowly high school dropout always made such gatherings uncomfortable. Mary was always quick to support him – how he dropped out to take care of his mother in hard times and fashioned a living working several menial jobs as a mechanic. 'If there was a busted car engine anywhere on campus, Luke could fix it.' she would proclaim. Even when Luke later confided in Mary that some of his sources of income were less than reputable, when some of those play-hard, party-hard students came knocking for a spliff or two, she was accepting.

Then there was the intellect. Mary had excelled at every level of academia, always several steps ahead of classmates, and frighteningly diligent for a twenty-two-year-old. When Luke's mother was going through the worst of times following her divorce, and having to adjust to independent living in the United States, it was Mary who was the sage, offering local guidance and counselling groups with no hint of reward. 'My father was the same …' she would say, '… moping around the house when my mother passed, despite being fully prepared. Truth is, no one's a one-man army.' Then typically she would follow this up with a reference to a famous victory by a recognised war hero, adding factual content to the legend. Her studies in Global History were being put to good use.

Luke pulled up to the kerb in his old rattling Jeep Cherokee, a work in progress. Mary trotted over, laughing alongside Jenny, her closest friend and nearest rival when it came to collegiate swimming. Hair still damp and filling the car with a musky chlorine smell, Mary leaned in for the welcoming kiss on Luke's cheek – 'Waiting long? Sorry … busy this morning and Jen and I were waiting for showers. Everyone gearing up for regional trials next week I suppose.'

'What distance you gunning for this time?' Luke asked as he checked his mirrors.

'50m front crawl, 100m front crawl … not sure about the 200m.' Mary replied, hastily applying a small amount of mascara using his rear-view mirror, before passing it back to Jenny, who sat behind her. 'It's getting close between me, Jen and Simone – could be anyone's game.' she chuckled.

'Simone's got nothing on you over 50m.' Jenny pipped up.

'Nor has she on you over 200 metres.' Mary commented. '100m though ... gonna be touch and go, girl. *Touch and go.*' The two sucked through their teeth and continued to exchange some playful banter.

'Sorry hun ... how's Elaine?' Mary broke in for a moment.

'Yeah, she's good Min, pretty good.' Luke nodded, using Mary's pet name, taken from a pink dress with white polka-dots she was wearing the night they both met at a local frat party. Mary 'Minnie Mouse' Cassidy stuck with everyone.

'Please tell me you got her a birthday present?' she said anxiously.

'Does a cup of coffee count?' Luke mocked, much to Mary's displeasure.

'Luke Allen. You are a *nightmare*.' she snapped playfully. 'Let's stop off at the mall down the road ... Jen and I need breakfast and you can go around the shops and find something.'

'Like what?' Luke protested.

'I don't know ... use your imagination. A card at least. What did your dad use to give her?'

Luke fell silent for a second while pretending to be distracted by the road ahead. 'Really can't remember.' Sensing she'd gone a little too far by mentioning his wider family, Mary backed down and extended the silence before Jenny chimed in again about coupons for Denny's she'd just found at the bottom of her purse.

Pulling into the mall, the trio made their plans for the next few hours. 'Jen and I will head off to Denny's,' Mary said, excited at the thought of a cheaper than usual meal. 'There're some jewellery shops on the first floor you can look at ... not too pricy. Oh. Get her a pair of earrings. She really liked the ones I was wearing the other day.'

Luke gave another nod, acknowledging the suggestion as Jenny headed in the opposite direction.

'Sorry about mentioning your dad.' Mary said, giving Luke's shoulder a soft pat. 'I just don't know why you don't try and speak to him, that's all.'

'Nothing to say.' Luke shrugged.

'What about your brother? Not spoken to him in ages?'

'Been busy I guess.'

Mary dropped her enquiries and gave a little peck on his lips. 'Love you Hun! See you in a bit.' She turned and followed Jenny before looking back. 'And don't be too long. Fireworks start at 6pm and Jen and I need to get ready.'

Luke took his place on the escalator, his mind now racing on the subject of family ties. Eight years, he counted, since he last spoke with his little brother, probably around about the same time he had last conversed with his father – and from what he could recall, it had been quite a heated discussion. Divorces are never the easiest of things to try and balance, especially when there's three thousand miles of ocean between the two sides. All Luke could recollect was a half-hearted offer of money from his father, which was promptly rejected out of spite, and his mother too tearful to even brave the phone, finding solace for missing her younger son's sixteenth birthday by opening another bottle of Jack Daniels.

A quick riffle through the dollar notes in his wallet brought Luke back to the task at hand. A small photo fell to the floor as he took out a twenty, jolting a memory. He, Mary, Jenny and a group of other friends had taken over a small photo booth at a party last Christmas, producing a strip of passport-sized shots of all of them pulling childish faces and dressed in suitably jolly attire. Mary embracing her nickname with the same polka dot pink dress, complete this time with mouse ears and glittery pink tinsel boa. Luke sporting a dodgy-looking stick-on white beard borrowed from some mall Santa that clearly didn't fit, with Jenny poking her head up from the back, donning reindeer antlers. It was enough to bring a warm smile to Luke's face again ... then he turned the photo over and read the mobile number hastily scribbled on the back. Jenny's number.

Careless in his selection of earrings for his mother, Luke strolled back down in good time, Mary and Jenny already waiting for him by his jeep. Mary inspected Luke's purchase and gave tame approval.

'Drop me off first, Hun ... got a few more pages to finish on my assignment for next week. Been driving me crazy.'

'You still coming out later?' Jenny asked.

'Of course girl. Don't you worry.' she smiled. 'You OK to drop Jenny off too, Hun? She's only around the corner.'

'I know where she lives,' replied Luke as he pulled up in front of Mary's dormitory.

'Should be good to meet around five-ish? Plenty of time.' Mary said, as she dug through her swim bag for house keys. Another kiss on Luke's cheek and she was out, jogging to the front door. Jenny switched up to the passenger seat.

Luke and Jenny exchanged a friendly but slightly awkward nod to one another as he pulled away.

'So, you looking forward to the regional trials?' Luke said to break the silence.

'I guess. Not sure I'm enjoying it as much now ... other things on my mind.'

'Yeah? Like what?'

'You know what.' Jenny replied bluntly. Luke fell silent once more.

Jenny's flat, which she shared with her aunt, came into view on the left corner of the road. Luke pretended to clear his throat as he slowed just by the lamp post.

'Guess I'll see you later?' he said flatly.

Jenny cast a glance in the opposite direction, in thought. 'Are we ever going to talk about this?' she responded, with a slight tremor in her voice.

'Jenny – look. This isn't fair, not on Mary.' Luke responded firmly as he went to place a comforting hand on Jenny's forearm. 'I think you're great ... really, I do, but I love Mary, you know that.' He had only just finished when Jenny threw herself forward to him in an embrace, gripping the back of his black leather jacket tightly and nuzzling the side of his neck. In an attempt to comfort her, Luke put his arms lightly around

Jenny's shoulders, followed by a few reassuring pats against her long blond ponytail.

His kindness was misread. Jenny tilted her head back and brushed her rosy lips across his stubble to meet his – the instant shock enough to paralyse Luke for a second or two before he forcefully pushed her away.

'Jeez, Jenny! What the *hell?*' he said, hands raised in emotional defence.

'I'm … I'm sorry,' a wounded Jenny replied, fists clenched and breathing deeply. Regaining her composure, 'I'll see you and Mary later, yeah?'

'Sure,' Luke agreed, still calming himself.

Jenny stepped out of the car, pausing just before reaching her front door, back turned to Luke, as a swift palm was raised to her eyes to wipe away any signs of tears, then opened and stepped in. Luke tightened his hands round the wheel and let out a sigh.

**Chapter 4**
**Bath, England**
15th July 2011 AD

Summer always drew out the best of the City of Bath. Its wealth of Georgian architecture played with the sunlight like nowhere else in Britain, the wide multi-storey terraces and crescents offering welcome breathing space from the swell of tourists that descended upon it. They soaked in the usual sites– the Roman Baths, the Abbey and the picturesque view of the Cotswolds from the tip of Sion Hill – along with the now familiar displays of medicinal salts and potions adorning every other shop window. It was also the best time to frequent The Rec, the City's own miniature colosseum to rugby, perhaps more integral to its people than the baths themselves.

The premiership season was over for another year, but action could still be found in the regular sevens series, pulling in locals but also visitors, no doubt attracted by the fanfare, with the promise of dry seating and absence of the usual mud. Adam had a somewhat obscured view of the action from the flat above the Bear Pub just north of the Rec, but could just see enough red and blue scarfs waving to determine what was going on, and in whose favour, if he leaned back far enough in his desk chair. He continued to thumb through the latest copy of National Geographic, attempting to digest what would have been an interesting article on the remains of Carthage if it had not been for the thoughts still whirling through his mind. Thoughts that had persisted over these past few months.

His earplugs were anchored in while he skipped through a mix of Oasis and Def Leppard, periodically getting up to pace while ruminating before returning to his desk. A firm knock on the door broke into his fragmented attention.

'You didn't go to the game?' Karen asked with surprise.

'No. Gave my ticket to Violet – she's not been in for a while,' Adam responded while wrapping the earplug cable around his iPod.

'Can imagine. Summer is always busy here – I don't know how she and Nick manage to run this place, being just the two of them. I've lost count of the number of times I've offered to wash up the pint glasses.' she smiled. 'How's the arm?'

Adam rolled up his left sleeve as evidence. 'Nearly gone,' he confidently responded.

Karen inspected further. 'Strange wound though wasn't it? Almost cauterised, as if by a hot blade? What did your father say?'

Adam pulled his arm away as if flustered. 'What he always says, *"You'll live."*,' rolling his sleeve back down.

'That's it? Despite your ability to heal he had nothing more to say?' came Karen's quizzical reply. Adam gave her an odd look ... of *course* he had more to say.

Interruptions came from downstairs, with the raucous welcome from Nick amid cheers of celebration. They were back from the game, Adam and Karen knew their cue.

'A win I hear?' Nick announced proudly, his arms up high, touching the top beam across the bar while allowing his barrel chest room to rest on the taps.

'Indeed. 26-22, and a fair match to the end.' William nodded with a wink as he hung up his Bath scarf on the hooks by the entrance and kicked off his boots onto the threadbare welcome mat.

'I take it young Violet cheered enough for the both of you?' Nick said with a hearty laugh, stained teeth breaking through his thick brown beard.

'Of course,' came the bouncy voice of Violet as she swept through, reaching just high enough to kiss her father on the chin. 'Rush will be coming, move out of the way!' in a more commanding tone, as she vaulted over the bar and readied herself for customers.

Adam and Karen had quietly made their way downstairs, Karen immediately hugging William before sorting his shirt out. 'Where's Richard?' she asked.

'Oh…just outside on the phone. Adam, your old man asked to see you.' William replied.

Anticipating such a request, Adam stepped outside, spotting his father pacing back and forth, mobile close to his ear. The conversation was fragmented, but the tone was serious. He hung up after catching Adam's eye and took a seat at a small wooden picnic table.

'That was Gary. He's in London. Apparently, a press conference is soon to take place outside the Cabinet Office …. not sure what he'll get but here's hoping.' Richard said, placing his staff by his side.

'Sir Lawrence set to be present I take it?' Adam asked. Richard just gave a nod.

'How's your arm?'

'Fine.' Adam wasn't going to go through the same routine as with Karen again, and knew his father was only being polite.

'Been out today?' Richard asked.

'No.'

'I need a walk. Knee is still playing up!' continued Richard, gently rubbing just above the joint. 'Come on. Will do you good … only so much you can get from staring at wallpaper!' he joked. Adam managed to raise a hint of a smile.

The sun had just crested below the hills of Coombe Down, providing enough soft glow to identify the footpath through Fairy Wood. Richard leaned heavily on his staff, puffing his way up the modest incline, Adam distracted by the odd bat swooping across their heads.

'Been practising?' Richard asked.

'A little,' came Adam's response.

'And …?' Richard pressed.

'And, what?'

Richard gave a now familiar heavy sigh once more while adjusting his lumbar with a stretch. 'You know what I mean, Son. Don't be coy.' Adam stared back for a moment before rolling his eyes, preparing for the lecture. The Sacred Band, descendants of the fiercest warriors of all Greece, abilities beyond compare thanks to the water from the Well of Ares..., his mind already interrupted by the almost exact same words coming from his Father.

'You've grown. This much is clear.' Richard continued. 'Libya proved that and Karen for one is certainly welcome to it.' He kicked his heel against a trunk to dislodge a pebble. 'Conjuring the shield is a good step. But what if that moment needed to be longer than just a single volley of bullets? What if you were faced with a relentless fire from all sides? Above? Behind? Defence is one thing, attack is another ...'

Adam interjected. 'I conjured it, didn't I? And I'm confident I could do it again ... but there's more to this than some pious Greek mythological magic, Father. Thank you for the loan of the pistol, by the way,' his response laced with sarcasm. 'Times have changed, we're fighting guns, not *spears*.'

Knowing he'd hit a tender nerve with his son, Richard backed down. 'Thank you for returning it.' he mocked, to dilute any tension. They took a seat on a fallen tree, taking a moment to admire the cityscape in the fading evening light.

'I'm not ignorant of my behaviour and what I ask of all of you.' Richard bowed his head pensively. 'You know what we face. What we've always faced. Myths and legends that parents would tell their children late at night always conceal an element of truth. That's what makes them entertaining ... but also, for us, remembrance is of vital significance.'

Adam would always recollect this sermon from his father, the childhood memories of him and his elder brother, having spent the best part of an hour before bedtime fussing over who got the top bunk, only to be settled down by their parents with a tale or two delving deep into Greek, Roman or alleged Arthurian history. Stories of warriors, conquerors and knights – some presented as fact, others as fiction – but all captivating to the imaginations of two young and courageous boys. There were times, he recalled, when his father would go too far ... too descriptive, too solemn. These were the times when their mother would react, the arguments would start and the only comfort the two got that night was the noise of their parents locked in verbal conflict downstairs.

There came a vivid sense of reality when Adam came out at the age of sixteen – no hesitation, no shame, especially after being brought up on stories of the legendary Sacred Band of Thebes. 150 male lovers, committed to their partners for life, given strength from the gods and goddesses of Olympus…. strong, courageous and indefatigably loyal. Everything a mother and father could hope for in a son. It was shortly after this that his mother and elder brother left for Boston, filling Adam with a sense of neglect and shame, swiftly remedied by his father. He did have a purpose – everything does.

Not long after this, more candid stories came from his father – the deeper, perhaps more sinister side that chilled his mother. Two factions at war, a round table divided, opposing views and versions of the past, present and future. Some would call it politics or alternative perspectives on history, but the Allen family knew better.

'I have to say, this might be a new record.' Adam spoke.

'What do you mean?' said Richard, now finding himself bat-spotting.

'It's been a good hour and a half, and you've not once asked me about my love life.'

A chuckle came from his father. 'I'm sorry. Clumsy of me.'

'Well, the answer is "No",' came Adam's obtuse response. For a short time, he used to believe his father was generally interested in his private life and what lay in store, and he was … partially.

'You know why I keep asking,' Richard said through a yawn. 'You think you are strong now? Just wait. The Band warriors never fought to win, but to protect. An instinct that will always prevail.'

The wail of a vixen was heard not too far off, and dusk set in. A skylark was visible from Adam and Richard's seating point, bobbing up and down in distraction from its grounded nest in hope of drawing any such predator away.

**Chapter 5**
**London, England**
**17th July 2011 AD**

'Red or green?' came a commanding tone through the small gap formed by a briefing room door left ajar. Tristan waited patiently outside, arms folded tightly and rocking on his heels. 'I'd go green, Sir. Less ... *aggressive*?' he passively replied while checking his watch. 'Sir ... I must hurry you. The press are waiting.'

The tall and slender frame stepped into the corridor, fidgeting with the double-Windsor knot under his chin and growling softly to clear his throat. 'Never been keen on green. Too regular. Morgan says I should never wear clothing that matches my eyes.' came a casual mutter as Tristan stood on tiptoe to assist with the suit jacket.

'Big crowd expected, I take it?'

'So-so. Mostly the regulars ... *The Times, Telegraph, BBC, ITV, Sky* ...' Tristan replied, brushing a few loose silver hairs from the shoulders.

'Standard government briefing?'

'I'd say so, Sir Lawrence. Just as we discussed. The National Libyan Army is a UK ally, agreed with our Canadian and French counterparts, NATO supported action, violation of human rights

'...' Tristan's commentary was trailing off when Sir Lawrence interrupted.

'What of Mr Hussin?' he said firmly.

'Mr Hussin, Sir?'

'Yes. Morgan said he was confronted while in Al-Khums?'

'Well ... yes, I believe he was, Sir.'

'By whom?'

'Still working on it, Sir ...' Tristan's stride was now having to quicken to keep up with Sir Lawrence's. 'Whoever it was ...'

'I believe you mean "Whoever *they* were", do you not?' came a condescending swipe back at Tristan.

'Yes ... well, possibly. We believe there to be at least two that evening.' Tristan stuttered.

'One trained in hand-to-hand combat, the other fierce behind the wheel of a 4x4 I hear? Evading armed forces? Well-read in archaeology? Deflecting bullets...? Is there anything I've missed Mr Baker?' Sir Lawrence's voice rose, hand gripping his cane so tightly the knuckles whitened.

The pair stopped abruptly, just short of the double entrance doors of the cabinet office, to exchange glances. Tristan gave a short swallow before composing himself.

'I know what you're thinking, Sir. Believe me we all do. We've been keeping the Red Dragon under surveillance for months now. Ever since your ... well, Lady Morgan's ... instructions. Those we are aware of.'

'Those we are aware of!' Sir Lawrence snapped at Tristan. He raised his thumb and index finger up to Tristan's eye line. 'We can be this close. This *close* … then lose it all! Fleeting moments, Mr Baker. Fleeting moments.' Sir Lawrence's tone began to rise again, only to be mellowed by the soothing, husky voice from behind him.

'Larry. Come now … not before interviews. You get far too tense.' Morgan's words tingled around his ear, instantly defusing his aggressiveness. 'You must forgive my husband Tristan; politics will be the death of him,' she smiled.

Tristan stood upright, his eyes unable to move from her own ash gray gaze holding him. He politely bowed his head in acknowledgement.

'Now. I trust you have been properly briefed, my dear?' she slid between the two men and cupped Sir Lawrence's face in her hands, his slight crack of a smile enough to earn an approving kiss.

'Good. Afterwards, we must talk. It's important.' She turned back to Tristan briefly. 'Alone if you please, Tristan,' once again supported with a tender look. Tristan again nodded before exiting through the doors to face the flashing cameras and relentless clamour of journalists.

'Another vision?' Sir Lawrence asked, drawing Morgan's hands down.

'More. An *instruction*.' She replied with enthusiasm.

'An *instruction* now?' Sir Lawrence sighed. 'We must be more certain this time my dearest. We can only take advantage of instability for so long … I can only take advantage for so long.' He continued pulling her closer.

'I always feel time is over-rated,' teased Morgan. 'Why should we of all beings be concerned about beginnings and ends?'

Sir Lawrence entertained her comments for a second before the pragmatist in him returned. 'Mr Hussin was confronted in Al-Khums. You know by whom. They are alongside us on the starting line my Dear, and we don't know which of us knows the terrain.'

Lady Morgan released a hand and brought it to her necklace, holding the pendant with care and falling deep in thought. 'I can see Larry. I can see it all. Long beaches, deep oceans, all of it. She will come soon. And She will have known love, known pain, and it will consume her. She will find me, find us, and it will be done.'

Sir Lawrence stood silent. These reveries from his wife were now becoming regular, almost to the point of incredulity, but something was different this time. He failed to identify what. He ushered her away from the doors and kissed her forehead, lingering a short while, seemingly unwilling to tear himself away.

'Albus Draco,' she whispered as she pushed him away dutifully, watching him stride through the doors, to be greeted by the same flurry of camera shots and shouts of 'Mr Worthington! Mr Worthington!' before they closed in silence.

**Chapter 6**

**North Atlantic**

**27th May 1941 AD**

The frenetic rubbing of hands was providing little in the way of warmth or comfort to Otto as he looked out across a chilly, whitewashed horizon during the early hours of the spring morning. Sleep still weighed heavy on his eyes following a night of panic below deck, desperately trying to correct severe damage to the Führer's flagship sustained from British Sopwith Camel assaults, her rudder permanently locked, forcing a near head-on collision course with a closing British Fleet.

The eruption of orders below deck to man every turret was of little interest to the twenty-year-old cadet, nor was the glory of the Third Reich, command of the seas or emergence of a new world order. His mission was clear, esoteric in its nature and certainly not for casual discussion with his crewmates over cold potatoes and porridge. A student of classics at Hanover University before the war began, Otto knew only too well the alignment between myth and fact, how empires rise and fall. Despite all the goose-stepping and sycophancy, Hitler's days were numbered, and Otto would be there when the statues were toppled.

But what would rise in its place? Which new phoenix, he wondered. Benevolent to begin with, only to metamorphose into bellicose evil like so many before? Championing a righteous cause at first, only to later reveal its true self? Forecasting became a woeful practice. 'Cassandra,' he often thought, what a truly awful curse … to see the very worst laid out in front of you and to have no-one believe you until it was too late. A cruel trick from the gods of Greece.

A warning siren bellowing across the ship sparked his adrenalin – '*Englisch! Englisch!*' spiked up from the decks below, amid a call to all stations. Watching from the portside, the ominous dark grey shapes of Royal Navy battleships pierced the line between sea and sky; a few more moments and they would be in firing range. Otto was still unfazed, however; the prospect of sixteen-inch shells raining down on them of little concern. His focus had been on another cadet, about his age, held in high regard by his superiors at least. Quiet amongst company, but always first to stand to attention and observe all the correct protocols. Little was known about him other than his birthplace just outside Munich and his family surname of Von Lamorak, which was often mispronounced as 'limerick', resulting in many poorly created renditions of five-line rhymes. Most had come to call him 'Mouse' as in 'Mickey Mouse', because of his first name Michael and his taciturn disposition. Otto had always found some measure of comfort in him though, opening up to reveal his own heartbreak at losing his lover Tomaz during the Polish conflict, and a shared indifference to the indoctrination of National Socialism – subjects that would certainly lead to severe repercussions against both should anyone else come to know of them.

Shells made thunderous splashes the height of trees as they began to fall within metres of their target. Boots thumped along the wooden decks as the crew desperately attempted to mount a response, primary gun turrets moving into position to salvo back, one of four now engulfed in flames following a quick direct hit to the bow. Otto tripped and fell down a small stairwell, covered his head with his arms amid the stampede, raised it just in time to see Mickey disappear below decks. He gave chase.

Darting through the mess hall, enduring rattling explosions reverberating through the ship and covering his ears to block out the endless sirens, Otto caught a glimpse of Mickey once more leaving his quarters, carrying a small object wrapped in cloth. That was it.

The two paused to acknowledge each other's presence before another blow to the upper decks knocked their feet out from beneath them, and a slow but steady list began to be felt. Adjusting to stand, Mickey bolted for the nearest door heading further into the bowels of the engine rooms. Otto caught his breath and followed.

Water had begun to seep through by the time he reached the engine room, hot steam clouding the view, and sparks bursting from every direction. Waving his hands to clear a path amid the acrid air, Mickey appeared again, coming to a halt in front of a small picture of the beloved Führer mounted thoughtfully on a rivet. They were immediately below the bow, tipping further and further backwards as the ship lost to the sea.

'Michael!' Otto coughed out. 'What are you doing here?'

'I think you know.' Mickey said with an unexpected stillness in his voice. 'What a dream our Führer had. What a vision. Like so many before him, only to be undone by those too ignorant to comprehend.' Mickey pulled from the cloth the object, a small statue less than a foot high, delicately carved in the shape of a woman ... the maiden.

Otto froze for a moment, all his suspicions confirmed. The relentless success of the Nazi advance, toppling the western powers like houses of cards; the capitulations, the massacres, all of it was true.

'You don't believe Hitler was going to let the pride of the German Navy loose into the Atlantic without results?' Mickey continued. 'He needed to make a statement, a success in the face of the British. My dear Otto, did you not see HMS Hood shatter into a million pieces only days ago? Churchill running scared? Europe overrun? All because of his vision, his *prize*.'

Otto glanced down at the statue, trying to shut out the increasingly maniacal ramblings of his crewmate as he edged closer.

'Please, Michael. Don't do this. Whatever you believe to be right, whatever your masters have told you, this power is not meant for us, for Hitler, for anyone. No empire born of the Palladium will ever end in peace for its commanders.' His hand reached out to take the statue from Mickey, but he read the move, responding with an assault with a wooden baton concealed up his sleeve, catching Otto on the jaw.

Otto stumbled back into one of the engines, scalding himself in the process as Mickey took a defensive position, left foot back, baton held high, the statue on the floor, defended by his feet.

'*Lies.*' he cried. 'The only weapon of the *ignorant.*' In a blink the baton transformed from wood to sharp steel, elongating to twice its original length, and requiring much of Mickey's strength to hold it aloft.

'Michael … it's over. Can't you see? Look around you. The ship is doomed. So is all of Nazi Germany.' Otto protested, still standing unsteadily as more direct hits landed above. Mickey was not deterred though, and lunged into a strike with his blade, splitting the iron beam at Otto's side when he dodged. He lunged again, slicing nothing but shadow, as Otto rolled out of reach behind him.

Otto took his own stance on Mickey's third strike, the shimmering shield of blue effectively rebuffing the sword sending out sparks. Otto knew he was not going to emerge the victor in an evenly matched battle with a pure blood White Dragon, and while hurling a swiftly conjured flaming blue spear over Mickey's head, he was preparing for sacrifice. Sacrifice for his mission, for his family, for Tomaz.

The pace of the water entering the hull had quickened from a steady stream to a full gush as more shells whined above. Screams of despair could be heard as the temperature edged up from the contained flames swelling inside the ship's boilers. An explosion threw the two of them against the metal wall almost in sync, splashing down into the now knee-deep pool in which they now found themselves. Mickey again rallied with a frenzied attack, possessed by fury, bringing the tip of his sword within inches of Otto. Otto leapt and gripped the pipework above, securing himself out of reach from the blade and landing a solid kick to Mickey's temple, knocking him face down into the water once more with a splash.

Otto released his grip and landed neatly, the water now up to his waist. His rival was already getting back on his feet, sneering through the soaked strands of brown hair partially covering his face. His teeth were clamped as if to make one final charge at Otto, undone by a flash of light behind him as another British shell crashed through the ceiling, debris crumbling down amid the explosion. Otto summoned his shield once again for an instant, just enough to propel him backwards ten metres or so, landing heavily on his right shoulder. In a daze, he looked back through thick, tarry smoke, expecting Mickey's sword to pierce right through it, but … nothing.

Straining for breath, Otto choked his way towards a faint whimper, the smog cleared by single beams of light now streaming through the gashes ripped through the battleship's hull. Mickey was alive, a shard of deck wood and metal lodged deep into his gut, his blood mingling with the froth of saltwater and oil. There was no saving him, but Otto could at least provide honourable comfort as he waded over and took his hand, clenching it tightly while Mickey's eyes glazed over before uttering his final words – 'Albus Draco'. The rising water took his head, then enveloped him completely. Otto pulled the cold hand close to his lips in a moment of grief, noticing the silver ring that first drew his attention to his crewmate several months ago – the same last words of Latin – 'White Dragon'.

There was still some headspace to breathe, but so little time now. Otto winced as he attempted to tread water, his right shoulder pulsing with the pain of his fall. He dipped underwater and frantically swept his hands across the floor, searching for the statue, but found only wreckage. He dipped, again and again, each time upon resurfacing finding less and less headroom to catch a breath. A final effort and his fingers grasped the unusual shape of the treasure, surprisingly heavy, as he hauled it to the surface and tight to his chest. There was no way out. He was pinned in a corner, watching walls become ceilings as the ship listed further. Water fought its way into his mouth and eyes, but while every survival instinct was there, Otto felt a need to release, completely let go. Nothing more needed to be proven – he knew it, Tomaz knew it.

**Chapter 7**

**Boston, USA**

**12th July 2011 AD**

Lucky goggles. Check. Lucky shammy towel. Check. Old torn costume from first regional collegiate relay win that really should have been thrown away years ago, but somehow can't let go of the superstition. Check.

Mary liked to be packed and prepared for everything and anything before competition day. She busied herself between the bathroom and the sitting room, stuffing items into a seemingly bottomless swimming bag while Luke lay stretched out on the sofa flicking through mid-morning television chat shows.

'My Crimson, Luke? Have you seen it?' she asked sharply.

'Your what?'

'My *Crimson*. You know ... sports top? Big 'H' on the front? Colour a bit of a giveaway?' she part-joked, part-snipped in response.

'Not seen it.' came a lazy reply. 'Tried the washing machine?'

Mary gave a subtle tut of disapproval before doubting herself and double-checking the washer. Sure enough, there it was, bundled up among some damp T-shirts and underwear. 'Found it!' she shouted, not willing to admit to Luke's triumph.

The bag was zipped tight and thrown over her shoulder. 'Right. I'm off to pick up Jenny. We'll be back later in the week. Promise you'll call me? Let me know Elaine's alright?' she prattled on as she scanned the room for her car keys.

Luke went quiet for a second upon hearing the mention of Jenny, then playfully grabbed Mary's arm. 'I might even call you because I *want to*.' he smiled, caressing her hips.

'Hmmm ... such a gentleman!' she conceded with a kiss. 'Be sure to record that interview with Ryan Lochte on USPN tonight, Babe. Don't want to miss it before the world champs start next week.'

'Uh-huh.' Luke noted.

'And before you ask ... yes, you're just as cute in Speedos." she shouted while heading out of the door.

Luke sat upright and watched her pull out of the drive with her usual beep of the horn as farewell. His smile soon soured as thoughts turned to Jenny and how things had been left between them. His mind wouldn't shift from the image forged only last week in his jeep, her crestfallen face as he spurned her advances. He wanted no trouble or pain, certainly not between Mary and her best friend on account of him. He settled himself, confident he had done the right thing, even confident enough to pull out that same Christmas photo of them all, with only a fleeting thought of calling Jenny's number on the back. He was fine. She would be fine.

✦    ✦    ✦

Mary pulled over and sounded her horn again outside Jenny's house, spotting her aunt waving from the upstairs window. Jenny appeared, matching swim bag in tow, still tying her hair up.

'Hey, girlfriend. You ready for this?' Mary beamed. Jenny gave a weak smile, almost awkward, before dropping into the passenger seat. The conversation was dominated by Mary from the first turn of the car wheel – pacing tactics, stroke technique, ones-to-watch – all the while trying to tune the radio to a station she liked. Jenny absorbed most of it, giving the occasional monosyllabic response while watching block after block roll past the window. She couldn't concentrate on Mary or her light-hearted discussion despite trying desperately. She was boiling with emotion, her heart was pounding, beads of sweat forming – she couldn't stand it.

'Minnie ... ' she interjected while Mary was mid-flow. 'How's Luke? Is he ... is he OK?'

'Luke? Yes, last time I checked. Why?'

Jenny went pale, stared down at her lap. 'Has he said anything? Anything about ... about me?' she stuttered.

'About you? No. Should he have done? What's up?' Mary quizzed.

Jenny continued to look down submissively, picking at her nails and trying to regain some composure. 'It's just that ... well, something happened. Last week, before we went out to see the fireworks.'

'What?' Mary asked, now frowning.

'We ... no, *I* did ... I did something stupid. Really stupid. I never meant to ... I mean *we* never meant to ... ' Jenny was stumbling over every word.

'Did what? What did you do, Jen?' Mary persisted.

'It didn't mean *anything*.' Jenny blurted uncontrollably. 'I promise. We only kissed ... just for a second. Then it was over!' she continued, as if weights were being lifted off her. The silence that followed felt like a trial by jury.

'*We* kissed? Or *you* kissed?' Mary broke, for the first time showing signs of restraint in her voice.

'Does ... does it matter?' came Jenny's naïve response. Mary again fell silent, then erupted.

'Does it matter? *Does ... It ... Matter?*' she cursed. 'My best friend kisses my boyfriend and she cannot distinguish whether it was mutual or forced?'

'No, no! I didn't mean that ...' Jenny backpedalled. 'You must have known how I've felt about him for all this time now. I just didn't know how to tell you.'

Mary was biting her lip. Despite the shock of confession, she had known. Perhaps she chose to bury it, not risk losing a close friend in exchange for the love of a man. She could bear this burden she thought, pay it no attention, it will ease and fade like a rash ... just don't scratch it. But now she had been cursed with the truth, she couldn't face it, she had no defence, only anger.

'How long? How long have you felt this way about him?' she fired.

'I don't know. Months maybe?' Jenny replied weakly.

'And does he feel …' Mary almost couldn't bring herself to ask. 'Does he feel the same way?' Jenny couldn't muster a response, only a slight shrug of her shoulders. Mary's typically sanguine composure was slipping.

'This all makes sense.' she retorted. 'Whenever Luke and I spend time together, you're there. You're *everywhere*. Can't get a moment alone. Well … now I know why!' her rant continued.

Starting to muster a defence, Jenny shot her friend a frown of disgust. 'What do you mean "I'm always around"? Maybe he's fed up with you *not* being around. Always studying. Always swimming. Always taking more interest in his drunk mother than asking about him!'

'Don't you dare bring his mother into this!' Mary rasped while pointing her finger directly at Jenny, completely unaware she had just run a red light. 'Your parents might not give a damn about you, but don't you dare try and drag everyone else down with you … .' She got no further. Mary's words, hot with hate and deliberately hurtful, were cut short by the booming sound of a truck horn. Just enough time was granted them to catch a blurred glimpse of headlights crashing into Jenny's side door. Glass showered them as their world turned upside down.

Mary flicked her eyes open. She could hear panicked voices from outside the car, calls for help and the faint smell of fuel. She tried to move but couldn't, legs trapped under a crumpled dashboard, seat belt still firmly in position. She gave a soft cry of distress but could summon little more. She twisted in her seat, still processing the topsy-turvy view of the outside, aiming to reach over to Jenny. She called her name with no response. She called again, but still nothing. Only when she successfully repositioned her body could she see … the blond hair matted with blood oozing from a gash on the forehead, eyes closed, mouth open a fraction as if to speak a final ill word towards her, only to be snatched away.

**Chapter 8**

**Bath, England**

**5th November 2011 AD**

There were deliberately no round tables in The Bear Pub. Richard had always been against them despite Nick's vocal opinion they created a friendlier atmosphere and encouraged conversation amongst his customers. The only exception to this was an informal briefing, deliberately kept away from anyone's home for anonymity, but also to take advantage of Nick's open tab bar.

'A success for democracy? That's how Larry put it?' Richard scoffed.

'Those exact words.' Gary confirmed, the pen in his hand running through his notepad.

'Any sign of Morgan?' Karen enquired. Gary shook his head.

'She would have been around. She always is.' William added, wiping beer foam from his moustache. Richard and Karen nodded in agreement.

'So ... another political skirmish in a foreign country. UK Government intervenes, prevents anyone else getting in or out on grounds of National Security, then leaves with full compliments from the United Nations and NATO, and makes everyone believe it to be a moral victory?' Richard concluded, slumping back in his chair.

'And a Nobel Prize coming for someone no doubt.' Nick joked from behind the bar.

'Well ... I don't think you'll find anyone sympathising with the Gadhafi regime. But I agree, it is an odd target for the White Dragon,' Gary continued.

Richard leaned forward, hands cupping his chin. 'Is it? Think about it ... Libya is one of the few countries that still celebrate Athena and Pallas, a festival of honour and love. Perhaps not in the ways witnessed during antiquity, but still ... Al-Khums is not a bad place to look for clues.'

'And if what we believe to be correct, that Lady Morgan has indeed lost sight of the Palladium after all these years, ancient folklore might just be all you have at this point.' Karen submitted her evidence to the group.

'There was everyone thinking Oppenheimer brought about real world peace,' joked William, earning a few chuckles from his friends.

Adam and Violet had remained outside the circle, entertaining themselves on the retro Pac-Man game Nick had installed in the corner, Violet concentrating hard on beating Adam's record score. 'You're toast, man!' she mocked as the points racked up. Adam took a low level of interest, constantly distracted by his father's discussions, picking up fragments.

'How long do you think it'll be before he calls you over?' Violet smiled.

'No idea. Bets are off this time,' he replied. Adam knew that since he and Karen had been in Libya his father, and indeed all his companions' nerves, had been on edge. Crossing paths with a White Dragon member so openly, far from home and apparently in a guise clever enough to infiltrate an entire North African rebellion. In past missions, results had largely been benign – the odd questionable encounter with some local, strange occurrences in places you wouldn't necessarily expect, be it in Iraq, Syria or Afghanistan. All sadly familiar with war, all equally connected with what was once Alexander the Great's empire. While no one was naïve enough to think such atrocities were the direct result of some divine intervention or mythical force, the pattern did raise questions, whether indeed their rival faction had forged itself a new role at the highest levels of government.

'*Adam.*' Richard beckoned his son over. There it is, he thought. Violet raised an inquisitive eyebrow as if to say 'Don't let him bully you.'

'Father?' Adam stood to attention, quite why he wasn't sure, but something about the presence of the other Red Dragon members all focused on him gave him reason to be more formal than usual.

'Please sit, Son. Now … about this assailant, Mr Hussin, in Al-Khums. You're sure he wasn't carrying a blade before engaging with you?'

'Confident, Father. He only had a staff.' Adam used his hands, over a metre apart, to illustrate, 'About this long.' Karen backed him up with a firm nod before looking back at Richard.

'From wood comes a blade.' Richard tutted. 'Hard to ignore, would we not all agree?' The table murmured in accord.

'So, what now?' Karen asked, addressing the whole group.

'The White Dragon don't have the Palladium. We would know it by now, surely?' Gary chimed in. 'Lady Morgan may have the necklace, but it's clear the guidance it's rumoured to give is failing.'

Richard appeared perturbed by this. While he could well believe that Lady Morgan, after centuries of wearing the fabled Necklace of Harmonia, could well have had difficulty in interpreting its power, she had kept a firm grip on the Palladium's whereabouts, skilfully passing it to the right bloodlines or those that best suited her and the White Dragon acolytes. Conquest after conquest, empire after empire, from Byzantine to British. Witnessing the chaos that followed each gave her almost the same pleasure as basking in the glory of their rise. Some may have called it a sardonic method of societal balance; Richard and his generations always saw the very worst – an unmitigated escalation to absolute power.

'Let's all be on our guard,' Richard concluded. 'While I agree with Gary, it is entirely possible Morgan has let her composure slip, she's clearly got reach – a support network beyond what we feared. Resources that certainly dwarf ours … even with the Sacred Band,' came his warning. Adam's ears pricked up at the mention of his brotherhood, often forgetting that its descendants from ancient Thebes could be anywhere in the world right now, but not know it—all three hundred of them.

'Are we still going to the charity ball this evening?' William switched topics as they all stood.

'Probably worth it.' Richard noted. 'It's rare for Mr Worthington to make an appearance on our doorstep with an open invitation. It's on the grounds of Newton Park is it not?'

'Yes … and if Larry Worthington begins prattling on about the common good in aiding children across the globe I might well get up on the stage and punch the son of a … .' Nick's grumbling was soothed by Violet's hand on his. 'Perhaps you'd best sit this one out, Dad?' she observed.

'Good idea. Adam – I'll need you though to accompany William and me. Just in case you spot this Mr Hussin chap,' Richard ordered. Adam agreed with reluctance before returning to his upstairs study. Violet caught his arm. 'You really don't want to go, do you?' she asked rhetorically.

'How could you tell?' he replied drily.

'Cheer up. There'll be fireworks at least.'

'Great,' came his sarcastic response at the thought of having to arch his head back to see this, when he could get a better view from the window in his room.

✦ ✦ ✦

The evening set in early. There was no formal dress code for the charity ball, but Adam did his best to squeeze himself into an old white satin shirt that had shrunk in the wash, and even buffed his shoes to a shine. Richard and William were waiting for him outside as they took the short walk over to the Newton Park campus just outside the City. There was already a line of cars queuing at the main gate when they arrived, and a few security checks. Gary greeted them there with tickets obtained through his connections with the *Bath Chronicle*. A temporary marquee had been set up just in front of the manor house, illuminated in delicate pinks and blues – just the right hues for a philanthropic children's cause. A photograph of Sir Lawrence Worthington MP and his wife Lady Morgan, both looking stilted as they stood with a group of orphaned girls and boys, stood proudly at the marquee's entrance. Huddles of guests gathered round it, exclaiming over its two founders and their unprecedented success around the world in providing love and warmth to those that would have had none.

'Capability Brown, I believe?' William said.

'What?' Richard replied, still scanning the crowds for any familiar faces.

'The manor house. Capability Brown's doing I recall … much like all of Bath,' William clarified, clearly taking no interest in the photograph.

'Don't really need a history lesson right now,' snorted Richard as he forcibly lowered Gary's camera to not to draw too much attention, before ordering him to get as close as possible to the stage. 'See if you can bring Sir Lawrence our way after whatever bombastic speech he gives. Be good to get a few questions of our own in.' Gary nodded and gently pushed his way through the crowds to the front, Richard and William taking aisle seats at the back, laying both their staffs on the floor.

'What should I do?' Adam enquired.

'Take a quick look around. Inside the manor house if you can. Anything we can use. If you spot this Mr Hussin chap come back here at once – don't engage. Understand?' Richard instructed firmly. Adam raised an incredulous eyebrow before stepping outside the marquee, just as the stringed quartet began to play an introduction for the evening's hosts, Sir Lawrence and Lady Morgan, and they were showered in applause.

'Thank you. *Thank you.*' Sir Lawrence took to the podium, forcing a wide smile while absorbing the camera flashes. 'No, please, dear ladies and gentlemen … this evening is not about me, nor my darling wife Lady Morgan. No. We are here tonight to celebrate all that is just in this world. Compassion, aid, and infinite love towards those innocents from all countries who may never have experienced what so many of us take for granted in our daily lives.'

The melodrama was already prompting growls of disapproval from William as he struggled for legroom with the row in front. Richard's eyes were firmly on Lady Morgan, poised and elegant as always in a shimmering silver gown and minimal makeup, and barely registering a hint of emotion while her husband took the limelight. The occasional punctuation of applause throughout Sir Lawrence's speech caused her necklace to catch the light with a flicker of ruby-red. Richard's eyes narrowed with intensive thought.

✦ ✦ ✦

Adam casually strolled up to the manor house entrance, which was flanked by two doormen. He gave them a lukewarm grin before asking them whether he could use the toilets inside for a moment, a plausible enough excuse to enter. Newton Park had been used for academia for the best part of fifty years, undergoing a great deal of change from the ground's fourteenth-century beginnings as St. Loes Castle. Lecture theatres, science labs and the students' union found their home somewhere on the vast campus. He took a wrong turn while trying to find the library and found himself in the on-site restaurant, filled with catering staff preparing canapés and drinks for the guests outside. Adam raised his hands in apology after drawing the gaze of several waiters dressed in black tie before swiftly turning back, accidentally knocking the elbow of someone holding a tidy tray of champagne flutes.

'I'm so sorry!' Adam blurted, attempting to steady the man.

'Not to worry, lad. My first day at this,' came the response in a comforting Irish accent. Adam took in a sharp breath as he measured him up – ash blond hair cropped at the sides and back, tall, well-built, slight stubble, about his age he would guess. A few seconds passed before he regained his composure and calmly asked where the toilets were. The man pointed down the corridor and to the left, leaving him with a wink. Adam followed the gesture, all the time aware that the man was still watching him as he left.

Once certain he was out of sight, Adam trotted upstairs in search of the library, taking the correct turn this time. Modern shelving stored many well-used books and magazines, neatly catalogued, with several grey desks and upturned chairs filling any empty space. A book, preserved in a small glass case in the corner, caught his attention – delicately bound, pages pristine – the title, *Wreck of the Titan: or Futility*, embossed across its cover in gold. A novella by Morgan Robertson.

'Still not found the gents then, Lad?' came that same Irish voice from behind. Adam spun around. He had been followed.

'Err … no. Sorry. Like a maze in here, isn't it?' he rebuffed, acting as normal as he could.

'Ah … interesting book that,' the man noted, walking over. 'Remarkable really. An act of complete clairvoyance. Only fourteen years out – poor buggers.'

Adam struggled to put the gentleman's comments in context before taking a closer look at the cover's illustration – a four-funnelled transatlantic liner. The publication date read 1898. 'Indeed.' Adam acknowledged, subconsciously noting Lady Morgan might well have been putting her powers to some use, albeit cruelly.

'Sorry, Lad, should have introduced myself. I'm Iain. Iain Donnelly,' the gentleman said, proffering a strong handshake. 'Guessing you're local?'

Adam nodded politely, still trying to assess Mr Donnelly. 'And you?' he enquired.

'Ah, Belfast, Lad. Me mam came over this way years back. Started in Manchester and just worked me way south I guess. Catering jobs and like. Makin' a livin' I guess. Worked for this Worthington lot for a few years now … bit up their own backsides but pay better than most,' Mr Donnelly replied, sinking both hands into his blazer pockets, completely relaxed. Adam attempted to mirror his demeanour while striking up more small talk, all the time conscious of what he had been sent to do in the first place. Their discussion was interrupted by the clap of a firework.

'Ahh ... looks like I'm needed.' Mr Donnelly noted. 'I'll be seeing you around, lad.' He followed that with the same casual wink he had made earlier. Adam smiled again before making his way back to the marquee.

Sir Lawrence and Lady Morgan were doing the rounds of meet and greet outside as guests jostled to speak with them and wax lyrical about their achievements, while bonfire night brought the night skies alive. Adam slotted himself into the crowd once more and spotted Gary making a line towards the celebrated pair, notepad in hand. Hopefully, in a position to grill the two further, he thought. Still no sign of Mr Hussin or indeed anything overly incriminating on the Worthingtons.

Richard and William had remained in the same spot at the back of the marque, staffs now in hand, whispering into each other's ears. Richard caught his son's eye and beckoned him over.

'Find anything?' he asked.

'No. Not a thing other than a chatty Irish waiter,' Adam reported. He was about to go on when the rasping voice of Sir Lawrence interrupted.

'Ah! Mr Allen. Good of you to come. Always a pleasure to see the celebrated family of Bath make an appearance at quaint gatherings,' he said while clasping Richard's hand in both of his somewhat over-enthusiastically. Richard forced a smile.

'And Mr Wood, isn't it?' Sir Lawrence continued, turning to William. 'I must say, I've heard wonderful things about the work you and your family have contributed to the exquisite carvings of Bath Abbey. A skill passed down through the generations no doubt?' he purred in reference to William's profession as a local stone mason. William gave a slow blink, seemingly not concerned.

'I must say, Richard good sir, I've somewhat lost track of your family and its activities. There were so many were there not? Quarrying, shipping, paper? What is it that you do now?' Sir Lawrence took a condescending interest. Most of the locals in Bath knew the Allen family was a rags-to-riches story, making their wealth from mining limestone to create the Georgian towns and cities across Britain, while diversifying over the following centuries. Now sadly, little more than a strong name was left, and they were living off their inheritance of land and property.

'Academia,' Richard replied laconically, still void of expression apart from the slight tightening of his grip on his staff.

'Ah, good for you. You know what they say, those that can't and all,' Sir Lawrence pressed ... enough to make William's face turn bitter. Adam stood calmly behind them. The frosty atmosphere was broken by Lady Morgan.

'Now, now, dear. We all know the importance of understanding our history. After all, how can we possibly expect to influence the future without it?' she said, tucking her arm under her husband's. 'And we all know just how much Mr Allen has contributed to the undergraduate programme here on this very campus.' She soothed further, triggering an awkward grin from

Richard. 'Your wife, Elaine, wasn't it? Do you still hear from her?'

The question caught Richard off guard, and he lowered his head and pursed his lips. Mercifully, Adam interjected. 'She moved. To America,' he fired back confidently.

'Oh. I was unaware. Fresh start I'm sure. Adam, is it? Why Richard ... your son has certainly grown up!' she flattered. 'And am I right in saying you have a brother?'

'Had.' Adam corrected sternly.

Sensing she had touched the intended nerve, Lady Morgan drew back. 'Well, do wish them both our very best, won't you.' she said coldly while ushering Sir Lawrence away. By this time Gary had caught up.

'Damn!' he snapped. 'Sorry, Richard ... never managed to get a word in. How about you guys?'

'Nothing of use.' Richard replied, gaze still lingering on the pair as they continued to make their way round the guests. 'I suggest we go.'

The group turned to make their way out, only to be blocked by one of the waiters. 'Do excuse me, sirs. Drink?' came the same Irish accent Adam had spent most of the evening listening to.

'No thank you.' William replied, still heading for the opened flap of the marquee.

'Ah, 'tis a party after all, Sirs. All for a good cause. Are you sure?' Mr Donnelly pushed. William and Gary remained unmoved by the invitation and continued to exit silently. Richard and Adam would have followed had it not been for the waiter's follow up – 'Be surprised if you and Sir Lawrence didn't have much in common now, lads.' Richard paused and gave a knowing look to Adam, an instruction given without words, before leaving with William and Gary. Adam turned back and took a glass of champagne.

**Chapter 9**
**Boston, USA**
**15th November 2011 AD**

The summer months had passed by in a daze, melting into the mellow colours of a New England autumn. Any chance of brief vacation getaways to the Maine Coast, enjoying beach barbeques and chasing the surf, had vanished in the blink of an eye, and homes were now beginning to be decorated with ripe pumpkins and cornucopias.

As with every national holiday, Luke found himself playing the outsider. Some seasonal floral motifs would decorate the dining room table but little more, other than indulging in the traditional turkey roast. Snow had begun to settle on the roads outside, drawing out the local kids with their sledges, flailing about making snow angels, and constructing modest-sized snowmen. A relatively mild winter approached.

A Thanksgiving invitation was usually sent to Luke and his mother by Mary's father, and always accepted. Not this year though. Despite Luke's best efforts at reconciliation, Mr Cassidy had strictly forbidden it, always protective of his little girl. Jenny's funeral took place in the early weeks of August, a big turn-out from extended family and friends – even Jenny's own mother and father putting their differences aside briefly for the sake of celebrating her life, cut tragically short. Predictably they went their separate ways the moment the wake was over, leaving her aunt to suffer alone in her mourning. Occasionally Luke would stop by her house and peer through the windows just to check in – sometimes she would answer the door, rubbing away any tears from her red eyes, other times there was no response.

Money was getting tight once again. Word was spreading across the Harvard campus of Luke's alleged misdemeanour with Jenny, and he lost business for car tune-ups and quick fixes. Temporary jobs in local garages went some way to helping, but sadly nothing much. The gossip still tormented him though, friends of both Mary and Jenny confronting him outside diners and their regular spots, eager for blood and humiliation, to the point where Luke almost felt like simply confessing to acts he did not commit just to ease the other people's consciences.

When stories of Mary's fragile mental health started to circulate, Luke's guilt grew worse. Mary had never been known to be a violent creature, so when a rumour spread that during the first week of term she'd exploded in a fit of rage -- the consequences of which saw two fellow students flung from their chairs and slammed into a row of lockers -- his concern grew as did his scepticism. He wanted to know the truth; he was desperate to know the truth.

'Have you tried calling her?' Elaine asked tenderly. Luke responded with a nod, while scrubbing the engine grease off his hands in the kitchen sink. 'What if you asked to meet up? Just for a coffee?' she naively continued. Luke's nod turned to a shake of the head. 'Surely she can't just ignore you?' She turned, throwing her arms up in the air.

'You reckon?' Luke snapped, tossing the dishcloth angrily into the sink. 'Not said a word to me, Mom. Not a single word since Jenny's funeral. All I get is snippy little remarks from those dicks on campus she calls friends!' he ranted, as Elaine softened her stance and held him from behind.

'You need to keep trying, darling.' she said, resting her head on his back. 'She won't have given up on you.'

'I would have done.' Luke exhaled. He turned and picked up the keys to his jeep. 'I'm going down the store ... do you want anything?' Elaine shook her head as she watched him skulk out the front door, tripping over a discarded exhaust pipe he'd left on the step, resulting in a curse word or two.

Slamming the door hard, he spat on his hands to remove a few stubborn specks of oil and grease when his mobile rang – it was Mary. In a fluster, he overworked the phone screen when accepting the call, switching it to speakerphone. A curious noise echoed from the phone around his jeep -- a wail, like that of a banshee, before cutting out.

'Hello? Minnie? You there?' Luke asked frantically.

There was a moment of silence, then came Mary's timid voice – 'Luke? Luke? I'm ... I'm sorry. I don't know what's going on ... I'm scared. Really, *really scared*.' she wheezed through tears. Luke needed no more, flooring the gas and screeching out of the driveway.

The Cassidy home was colonial in its styling. Her father was recognised as a successful lawyer in the city, and he had invested heavily in its traditional features, sparing no expense. Luke cast his eyes up to Mary's bedroom window overlooking the sycamore in the front lawn. It was open, curtains billowing out slightly. He could hear her sobbing. It was enough to risk action.

He climbed up the frost-coated tree, reminiscent of happier times when he would sneak into her room to avoid interrogation from Mr Cassidy at the front door – always at Mary's request. He reached out just enough to lift the window sash higher and vault his way inside. In the corner sat Mary, curled up tight, face buried in her knees, rocking ever so slightly back and forth. Her room looked like a bomb had gone off -- school papers, books, even furniture thrown against the far wall. Fragments of ornaments and pictures lay scattered over the floor, except one. A framed shot of her and Jenny was neatly propped up in front of her.

Luke's instinct was to rush to her aid, throw his arms around her in comfort … but something was wrong. He could not place what exactly. A feeling of pain and anguish not of his own making surrounded him, seizing his muscles. He was cold, yet also sweating, as if suddenly struck by an illness. He looked at the bedroom door, hanging off its hinges, Mr Cassidy's leg propping it open as he lay motionless on the floor. Luke shook off his morose feeling and ran to Mary, holding her tight.

'Min? Minnie? What happened? Tell me?' he asked as softly as he could.

Mary could only continue to tremble, breathing sharply while trying to wipe away her tears and form a coherent sentence. In her hand was a crumpled leaflet – 'The Funeral of Miss Jennifer Van Hansen' -- together with the date. Luke tucked her head under his chin and called 911.

It took less than an hour for emergency services to arrive, whisking Mary and her Father off to the hospital, Luke in tow. Remaining remarkably calm, he got in a quick voice message to his mother and asked her to meet him there, eager to get a second opinion. He decided to keep Mary's other friends out of it for now, at least until they knew what they were dealing with. Elaine was already at the hospital entrance when they arrived, desperately resisting the urge to light up a cigarette to quiet her nerves. She embraced her son tightly, exclaiming over the tragedy while asking questions to which Luke had no answers yet. It wasn't long before the two were approached by the doctor, stern in expression and glasses perched on the tip of his nose, complete with a medical questionnaire. Luke and Elaine completed it the best they could on Mary's behalf, scratching their heads for any previous recollection of epilepsy or convulsions, stress or simply poor mental health. When she asked about Mr Cassidy, Elaine buried her head into Luke's arm upon learning he was still unresponsive in a coma.

It was no more than a few hours before the two received word from the nurse that Mary was up for seeing guests, although only for a short while, while the sedatives wore off. Luke and Elaine stepped into the side room to find her stretched out prostrate on what looked like a fairly uncomfortable hospital bed, an IV line hanging loosely from under her gown.

'Min? Can you hear me?' Luke whispered. Mary's eyes fluttered open and she let out a groan. 'Are you in pain? Where does it hurt?' Luke continued. Mary just slowly shook her head while trying to croak out a sentence.

'Dad? ... Where's Dad?' the words eventually struggled out. Luke placed a reassuring hand on her shoulder.

'He's going to be OK. You're going to be OK.' He said, not sure whether the doubt in his voice was noticeable. 'Can you remember anything? Anything at all?'

Mary looked directly up at the ceiling, still wrestling with consciousness. 'Jenny ... what happened to Jenny?' she uttered. Luke and Elaine could only look at one another for a suitable response.

'Jenny's ... well, Jenny's not with us at the moment, Mary.' Elaine comforted. 'I'm sure you'd like to see her ... we all would.'

'I've seen her. I *saw* her. Just now. She was in my room. Where is she now?' Mary protested, raising her voice. Luke and Elaine exchanged glances once more before Luke took her hand and patted it. 'I don't think she was with you, Min, not just now,' he said gently.

Her pulse began to quicken, the monitors flickered as if something was wrong, her breathing went faster. '*She ... Was ... Here.*' Mary screamed. Her anger escalated, the bedside table started shaking, her voice deepened to an almost unrecognisable sound. Luke continued to hold her hand, but that same feeling of sickness began to return to the pit of his stomach. Mary sat bolt upright in the bed and screamed loudly, bringing two nurses to her room. They swiftly restrained her and increased the dose of her sedative. She settled back into a shallow sleep.

Luke stood back, startled, turning to his mother who looked like she'd seen a ghost. 'I'm sure she'll be OK, Mom. Hell only knows what they pumped her full of in here.' he said softly.

Elaine stood motionless. 'Her eyes. Did you see her *eyes*?'

Luke looked confused. 'What about them?' he asked.

'We should call your father. Now.'

**Chapter 10**

**London, England**

**20th November 2011 AD**

Technology was not Tristan Baker's strong point. He was furiously tapping buttons on the remote that operated the large screen in one of the cabinet office briefing rooms. Victorian oak wood panels dressed the walls, on which baroque frames the portraits of military leaders of Britain's past – The Duke of Wellington, Horatio Nelson, Winston Churchill. The square glass table placed right in the centre of the room clashed with its antique setting. Those present helped themselves to glasses of water or cups of tea and coffee while Sir Lawrence Worthington sat at the head of the table, rattling his fingers on its surface impatiently.

'Any moment, Sir. Ah! Here we are.' squeaked Tristan as the screen came to life, revealing a room dressed in opulent fabrics and Arabic fixtures. Sitting in front of them was a well-dressed man, staff by his side, dark facial hair trimmed neatly.

'Mr Hussin. Thank you for joining us at such short notice,' Sir Lawrence began. 'I appreciate your work in Libya must be keeping you busy. It does not go unnoticed, I promise you.'

'Thank you, Sir Lawrence and my apologies, too. It has been some time since I reported in, but I'm sure you and your colleagues can testify to the fact that it has not been an easy few months out here,' Mr Hussin replied.

'Indeed, indeed. All the more reason for speaking now.' Sir Lawrence said. 'Let me start by asking how the excavation went at Al-Khums ... anything further to note?'

'Little, Sir. Aside from the intrusion I informed you and Lady Morgan of earlier.'

'Yes, yes ... interesting development. Can't say for sure how long Karen Wood had been tailing us out there, but mark my words, she and the rest of the Red Dragon are under constant surveillance,' Sir Lawrence reassured, turning to Tristan for confirmation.

'She was not the only one though, Sir.' Mr Hussin grumbled. 'The boy? Rather, the young man? What of him?'

Sir Lawrence shot a glare towards Tristan, who promptly raised a series of photographs for Mr Hussin's education. 'These were taken at a recent charity ball over in Bath. I believe this to be the young man you confronted?' he enquired. Mr Hussin leaned in closer to his webcam to inspect them, then gave a nod in agreement.

'A Sacred Band member we think.' continued Tristan. 'Son of Mr Richard Allen ... Adam, we believe. I'm sure you are familiar with the Allen family history?'

Mr Hussin gave a vigorous nod. The leader of the Red Dragon, chief descendant of Galahad himself, now entangled in an enterprise that had taken their counterparts many decades to build. Mr Hussin squirmed in his seat with agitation.

'We believe Karen ... or Mrs Wood -- not her real surname by the way -- was there acting on this Richard Allen's request.' Sir

Lawrence elaborated. 'She was in fact a Mrs Karen *Milligan*, local substitute schoolteacher, of the linage of the Knights of Kay.'

Mention of another Red Dragon member involved caused increased tension within Mr Hussin, now visibly twitching. 'Anything else I should be aware of, Sir Lawrence?' he replied sharply.

'William Wood, the stone mason from the city. Son of Gawain and close to Richard. Nick Butcher, son of Bors, and a landlord. Known about them for years,' came a chilling voice from the far chair. Flushed cheeks either side of a stout nose, thick neck almost choked in a tight-fitting military collar and tie, large hands placed firmly on the table.

'Yes, thank you Colonel Thorpe. We're also watching Gary Willis, the journalist. Still not sure about him, but he's been turning up at a few press conferences recently – most inquisitive fellow,' Tristan chimed in.

'So that's five … possibly six, Sir Lawrence? Tell me … were you ever planning to inform me and my men?' blustered Mr Hussin.

'Well, I'm sure the followers of Palamedes are more than capable of taking care of themselves,' Sir Lawrence flattered, holding his hands up in conciliation. 'Besides, rooting through a "Who's Who?" of our enemies was not the purpose of this meeting.' He stood, straightening his back with a click. 'Gentlemen. The visions of the Palladium, they are getting stronger. More distinguishable,' he announced. Tristan and Colonel Thorpe turned to one another, trying to hide any incredulity.

'As you are aware, all of you, Lady Morgan's visions have been somewhat clouded of late ... more wild stabs in the dark than precision,' he continued, circling the table as he spoke. 'We all know, we, our ancestors, loyal and righteous defenders of destiny, have shaped this world as we feel it should be – always a balance, a tipping of the scales when we see fit. It has served us well for many a century ... but these past seventy years have escaped us. Certainly, our influence has grown, my friends – a skirmish here, a famine there, enough to keep us relevant. But not to the just heights we ought to aspire to.'

Colonel Thorpe brought a large palm over his bald head and scratched. 'So ... what are you saying, Larry? Has your Mystic-Meg got her marbles back in the bag?' he said caustically. Sir Lawrence allowed his lapse of formality.

'I'm saying, Colonel, son of Gareth, that for the first time since the Second World War, we might be on the right path,' he confirmed with a sharp glare.

'No more visions of sand leading me into the Libyan Sahara dusting off old relics?' Mr Hussin said, the sound breaking up slightly.

'I'm sure you can understand, Mr Hussin, that it was only logical for Lady Morgan to search sites of the most primitive of folklore. Al-Khums was, after all, long celebrated for its festivals of Athena and Pallas,' Sir Lawrence clarified.

'So, where is the Palladium now?' Colonel Thorpe said firmly. Sir Lawrence took to his seat once more and revealed another photograph, this time of the Al-Khums site. He pointed to the carvings - the statue, circling it with a red pen. His guests looked puzzled.

'Gentlemen. I am sure you are well versed in the myth of Athena, goddess of wisdom, and the tragedy of her closest friend Pallas. The unintended death of her friend, the guilt that this cast over her, enough to even take up her friend's name in posthumous honour ... *Pallas* Athena. The Palladium was her tribute, and it stood in ancient Greece for many a century. An empire rises, only to fall.' Sir Lawrence became more animated with his hand gestures. 'Alexander the Great. Julius Cesar. Charlemagne. Troy ... well, the jury is out on that last one – quite possible though,' he shrugged.

'We know all this, Sir Lawrence.' came an ill-tempered response from Mr Hussin. 'Lady Morgan has held the Palladium for centuries, aligned to your own bloodline, that of Sir Lancelot himself. We of the White Dragon are indebted to your family, Sir, but as you say, appear none the wiser on recent events or your Ladyship's apparent inability to locate the sacred statue.'

Sir Lawrence puffed his chest and leaned on his walking staff, noticeable exasperation spreading across his face. 'Gentlemen. Lady Morgan believes Athena incarnate is among us.' He was met with a collective groan from his colleagues.

'We've heard that before, Sir Lawrence. Lady Morgan and your good self have spent many a year searching for this reincarnation ... how has the Orphaned Children's Charity been serving you?' came the acerbic response from Colonel Thorpe. Sir Lawrence absorbed the hit.

'Yes, yes, Stephen. I was fully anticipating your scepticism. But as Mr Hussin's work in Al-Khums has illustrated, it is likely not just a myth or legend. An almost hereditary line not dissimilar to our Arthurian roots, only more clandestine, harder to read or indeed witness in a lifetime. But ...' Sir Lawrence was again interrupted by a ghostly figure appearing from the shadows of the room.

'But seen before. Not always clearly, but now more lucid than ever before,' Lady Morgan presented with grace. Her arrival triggered all to rise to their feet in respect.

'My lady. You have long possessed the Palladium, bent it to our will, and for that we are grateful.' Tristan quivered obsequiously. 'But ... but, what makes you sure this time?'

Lady Morgan glanced down at her necklace, twisting the jewel to cast a slight gleam. 'Ares knew. Brother to sister. One will always find the other.' Her response caused further bewilderment to the group before Sir Lawrence helped clarify.

'My darling wife as you say, Tristan, has always kept the Palladium close to us. Created new worlds for us, and indeed, cleansed them when we needed. Since the Second World War we have been without a guide, as we have discussed. But the Palladium is never truly lost, not while the Necklace is still in our presence. One must always follow the other, you see?'

Although Sir Lawrence and Lady Morgan's description of events was striking a chord with their audience, they remained far from convinced. Such an irregularity, even despite their own lineage, but enough hope attached to endorse loyalty to their cause.

'So, how do we find this Athena incarnate? Assuming of course she knows the precise whereabouts of the Palladium,' the Colonel queried.

Lady Morgan sent a reassuring look his way. 'She will know. And she, Stephen, will find me.'

**Chapter 11**

**London, England**

**24th November 2011 AD**

The cold and bleak view across Heathrow runway was a far cry from how Mary would have wished to spend Thanksgiving. Little over a week had passed since her incident at home, the time being filled with appointment after appointment, meeting medical professionals, covering everything from blood work and MRI scans to counselling and bereavement therapy. All nonsense as far as she was concerned.

Luke had held her hand for most of the flight, occasionally sending a warm smile her way or touching upon some childhood stories from his time in the UK. She sensed he was as uneasy about this visit as she was, the thought of meeting his father again after so long, having to reignite a relationship with his younger brother, answering the same banal questions from everyone concerning how he's been after all this time, what life was life in America, whether he'd made friends and so on.

The plane taxied to a halt as passengers began to scramble for their hand luggage. 'You ready for this?' Luke asked Mary, still gripping her hand. Mary mustered the best facial expression she could in reply. She had spent most of the trip contemplating Elaine's words, her recalling of an incident that plagued her and her former husband before the birth of her two boys. A young girl from inner Birmingham, raised by

Pakistani parents, forced into an arranged marriage against her will. She loved another, a boy from across the street, meeting in secret under cover of darkness. She was spotted one night by her closest friend, a friend who swore she would not tell a soul about her indiscretion. But she was deceived, and later that month she would be confronted by her parents together with the father- and mother-in-law to be. The shame was unbearable, but so was the anger, the thirst for revenge over such treachery. She confronted her supposed friend in a local bar, things got heated, the argument spilled out into the street. Before anyone could act, the girl had pushed her friend into oncoming traffic in a fit of physical aggression – nothing could be done.

It was shortly afterwards that this same young girl began having what could only be described as seizures – powerful seizures, enough to shake the foundations of her family home. Irregular at first but then more common and increasing in intensity. About this same time, Elaine's husband Richard began making trips to Birmingham, acting on local knowledge and gossip fed through various sources – some reputable, others less so. Whatever it was, it was consuming much of his time and eroding their precious marriage. Elaine was always committed to her husband's exploits, no matter how farfetched they seemed, but this was different, almost harassment. When news broke that the young girl had taken her own life in a canal, the distance between Elaine and Richard widened to irreparable levels. The birth of Luke, swiftly followed by Adam, patched things up for a while, but sadly not enough to salvage the marriage.

Luke and Mary were ushered through customs check, all painless. In the main terminal they were met by Richard and Adam, both expressing some measure of gratitude at their arrival – more so by Luke's father than his brother. Mary cowered at first behind Luke as he got a welcome hug from Richard, a handshake from Adam, then they engaged in small talk about the flight and whether they were hungry. Richard finally stretched out his arm to embrace Mary lightly, to comfort her, before Adam again gave a sterile handshake to greet her.

An airport coffee shop satisfied everyone. Richard immediately dispensed with the pleasantries and started his interrogation. Mary tried to explain, often vague in her descriptions and fighting a touch of jet lag, supported by Luke when he felt his father had overstepped the mark. Tension within this family unit was all too clear, Mary thought, feeling very much like a relic to be examined and pondered over – just as all doctors and professionals had been doing for these past few days. It was tiring, it was frustrating.

'How's your mother?' Richard asked Luke, trying to switch topic.

'Fine.' Luke bit back. Richard enquired no further.

'Your brother here has been very busy of late. As have I. Sure your mother will understand why we've not been in touch,' Richard defended himself, wiping his mouth with a paper napkin. Luke gave no response, other than a glance of recognition towards his little brother.

'We'll head straight back to Bath.' Richard continued. 'You can catch up with everyone there – William, Karen, Nick. They've all been asking about you.'

'Nick and Violet still running The Bear?' Luke feigned interest.

'Yes. Very good job they're both doing, too. Offers much needed privacy. Adam's taken a room upstairs in fact.'

Luke was pleased to hear this. He always thought his brother would just end up rattling around the Allen house alone, swept up in his Father's antics and finding precious little time to himself. Bath was never the best place for a young gay man to grow up ... especially one indoctrinated with myths moulded within a reality set to persist into adulthood. The group left for the car park when Luke pulled Adam back out of earshot.

'You still caught up in all of this?' he enquired.

'Of course.' Adam managed to lift a smile. Luke rolled his eyes.

'What's he had you doing? Chasing more wizards and fairies?' he teased. Adam dismissed the jibe with a playful jostle.

✦ ✦ ✦

As Richard promised, almost everyone had gathered at The Bear when they arrived. William and Karen, arms locked together, thrilled to see Luke once more and complimenting his looks in comparison to his father. Nick and Violet turned their attention to a still isolated Mary, immediately making her feel more at ease. The brothers sought refuge upstairs to escape the further questioning, Luke immediately inspecting Adam's music collection.

'Struggling to shake the Brit Pop movement then?' he laughed.

'What were you expecting? Judy Garland?' Adam mocked back.

Luke continued to study the room, turning over National Geographic magazines, history books and the odd *Wikipedia* print-out on ancient sites and monuments. He came across a tourist guide to Libya and froze.

'Please don't tell me...! Seriously, Adam?' Luke probed. Adam nodded before making his excuses. 'Adam. These are *war zones*. Dad can't be sending you there?' Luke persisted.

'It was necessary. Believe me ... if you only knew what we have been up against, Luke. You would have done the same thing.' Adam justified. But Luke creased his face dismissively.

'Come on, bro. You know this is nonsense. It's an *obsession*. OK, were there Knights of the Round Table? Quite possibly. Are there any descendants? Maybe. But all this trash about higher powers and god-like interference in human affairs for years is a bit of a stretch, don't you think?' Luke challenged.

'If that were so, why are you here?' Adam stood his ground.

Luke looked down, struggling to find a suitable response, other than 'Mom told me to'.

Violet came knocking on the door. She informed the two that Richard intended to head for Glastonbury, Mary was going to join him. The thought of another trip so shortly after he and Mary had landed did not sit well with Luke, but he was beyond arguing when he saw everyone downstairs already making for their cars. He pulled Mary close.

'Your father is quite the fantasist, isn't he?' she smiled.

'Sorry. I know they can all be a bit much,' he admitted.

'No, not at all. All quite interesting really,' she replied. It would appear that Mary was actually more comfortable with this more unorthodox line of enquiry than the endless medical terminology she'd been hounded with recently.

+ + +

During the short trip down the A39 Richard was constantly monitoring his rear-view mirrors, clearly unsettled. Luke and Mary sat patiently in the back, eavesdropping on the conversation between his father and brother at the front.

'So. You're sure you can trust this guy, Adam? This waiter?' Richard asked.

'I believe so, father. He just knew too much. About things no ordinary person would know or care to know.' Adam replied.

'Hmmm. In which case, the White Dragon are quite possibly aware of our discovery. We might be being followed right now. Are you sure we can trust him?' Richard quizzed.

'I believe he's on our side, father, yes.'

'A Sacred Band member?'

'Possibly.' Adam gave a coy shrug, not unnoticed by Luke. Most considered his younger brother cold, emotionless, but Luke could always tell a charade when he spotted one from him.

'There's a *guy*?' Luke leaned forward. 'Sacred Band? You have been busy, bro.' he joked with a little punch on the arm.

'Knock it off, Luke.' Richard snorted.

'Why? I'm genuinely curious.' he continued to chuckle. 'Adam and his posse of warriors coming to defend the Earth!' the chuckle broke into a laugh. Adam just turned to look at the pleasant scenery from the window, not dignifying it with a response.

'I'm a *discovery*?' Mary interjected. Silence fell in the car. Luke dialled back and resorted to holding her hand once more. 'Luke? What does your father mean? A *discovery*?' He had no answer.

The Tor punctuated the knolls around Glastonbury, skies still grey and weeping. Its summit, crowned with the remains of St Michael's Church, would typically be covered by a swarm of tourists, but thankfully the quieter winter months offered the locals some respite. The cars pulled up alongside the George Hotel and Pilgrim's Inn, Richard stepping out briefly to brave the drizzle and knocking on its door. A lady answered and welcomed him in. No more than ten minutes passed before he returned and jogged backed to William's car, giving instructions. He jumped back into the driver's seat. 'We've got about an hour.' he claimed.

The cars stopped again, this time alongside the fabled Chalice Well. 'I know this place.' Mary said, continuing to recall travel tales of her college friends visiting the UK during festival season in the town and returning with kitsch gifts of Arthurian tea towels and miniature statues of Merlin. Everybody got out of the cars and made their way to the garden entrance; a guide was seen politely ushering the few visitors they had out, then acknowledging Richard with a nod as he waved their group through.

The gardens were delicate and tranquil as one might expect, with Mary admiring the trellis archway flora as Luke began to recite yet more childhood visits in his head. Little had changed.

'You can actually drink from that, can't you?' Mary asked as they walked past the Chalice Well.

'I wouldn't advise it. Stick to bottled.' Luke joked, as Mary walked over to inspect it.

'You remember my dorm mate Lisa during my first year at Harvard? Her late grandmother had a brooch with this on. Lisa never wore it herself, thought it old-fashioned, but always kept in in her jewellery box.' Mary smiled, pointing to the emblem on the hatch of the well.

'It's called a vesica piscis,' Karen interjected. 'Call it an ancient Venn diagram.' She continued with a grin. Richard walked over and urged them to sightsee later.

At the end of the garden stood an old brick wall with a shabby wooden gate. Richard pulled out an ordinary-looking Yale key and twisted it with some force in the rusted lock, springing it open. A narrow stairway appeared in the dark and damp, and William flicked his torch light on. 'Watch your step, everyone.' he warned.

Single file they descended, inhaling the heavy musky smell of the aquifer that ran deep. Luke left Mary in the care of Karen as he worked his way to the front alongside his father.

'Dad, what's all this about? Don't you think Mary's had enough to deal with of late?' he pressed.

Richard moved quietly for a moment before gently whispering to Luke. 'Your mother called me. Told me everything. I consider this necessary, yes.' he responded. Luke felt hurt that his father refused to elaborate further, and made his way back to Mary. So much of his and Adam's upbringing had been marred with secrecy, he thought now more than ever would have been a time for honesty, they weren't children anymore. He put his arm around Mary, who was starting to shiver with the effects of the subterranean cold, as Adam gave a small lecture on the meaning behind the vescia piscis -- how for many years it had been one circle rather than two, and the divergence of the round table still joined by the sword of Excalibur through its centre despite their apparent separation.

Richard halted the group at a small rocky opening, high above the water which trickled steadily onto a smooth flat stone. The roots of a tree were visible, entering from the top, and over time meandering their way across the walls of the cave in natural decoration. William, Karen, Gary and Nick took their places around the flat stone in apparent order, as Richard turned to Luke and Adam and suggested they wait further up the stairway with Mary. Luke sneered at the thought but gave in to Mary's insistence that they did as they were told. The three sat patiently a few steps back around the corner, Luke passing his jacket over to Mary to ease the chill.

'So, tell me about this guy?' Luke turned to Adam.

'It's not what you think,' Adam defended.

'What's he got to do with all this then? Why's Dad so interested?' Luke persisted. Adam provided a brief overview of the charity ball evening and the discussion with Mr Donnelly. All very formal, but something was amiss, Luke noted to himself – Adam almost breaking ranks to describe the waiter in more detail than was necessary, combined with pauses in his train of thought, as if distracted. His little brother had found more than just an intriguing lead that evening, whether he was prepared to admit it or not.

Richard's voice echoed through the stairwell, Mary catching snippets and the switch of voices as the others expressed statements and views. She wasn't overly well versed in the Knights of the Round Table, but did follow the way they addressed one another – the 'Sons of Galahad, Bors, Gaheris and Gawain, Daughter of Kay' – together with a few generic references to King Arthur and his legend.

'Percival'. Mary spoke suddenly, catching both Adam and Luke's attention. 'Wasn't there a Percival?' she enquired. Luke did a bit of a double take and started stuttering a clumsy explanation before Adam took control.

'There was indeed. He died a virgin. So, no descendants,' he stated, Luke firing back a look of disbelief at his pragmatic response.

'Oh. What about Lancelot? He a virgin too?' Mary quipped.

'No, very much still with us. Just not *with us*, if you know what I mean.' Adam replied, his nonchalance on the subject starting to irritate Luke. Adam's description began to click together with his earlier description of the vesica piscis, a once collective group of Knights now split, heading their separate ways, perhaps even in confrontation. She turned away from the brothers once again and tried to edge closer down the stairwell to listen in more.

'So, if this waiter, Iain, is a Sacred Band member, he's on our side, right?' Luke questioned Adam further.

'You'd like to think so. He certainly knew a lot about Sir Lawrence and Lady Morgan, their activities and connections. Not unheard of that the Band would deploy a spy,' Adam confirmed.

'Did Dad know anything about it?'

'Apparently not. But then, it's not like we all have Skype meetings every week to check in.' Adam managed to lighten the mood.

Mary had crawled to get within clear hearing distance of Richard's gathering, picking up more threads. Topics had shifted from Arthurian to ancient Greek – the Goddess Athena, God of War Ares, and a statue of destiny.

'Friends, let's not underestimate this challenge,' she heard Richard utter. 'Lady Morgan has, as we know, long held the Necklace of Harmonia, until recently the Palladium with it. Now, if Adam's source is to be believed, the latter may soon be finding its way back to her …. Combine this with Elaine's contact and the arrival of young Mary. You know, I am no fortune teller, but these are convergences that cannot be ignored.'

There were a few muted mumblings from the others before she heard William's voice. 'None of us are blind to this threat, Richard, nor do we doubt you. But you'll understand after what happened in Birmingham all those years ago, why some of us are reluctant to pursue this matter,' he said with some force.

'I know, I know ... but if anyone was to deter me, to deter us, it would be Elaine. Why would she nominate Mary if she feared the same scenario?' Richard countered. The gathering again mumbled, this time with a sense of approval.

'What do you propose?' came Karen's voice.

'It was clear from your and Adam's visit to Libya that the White Dragon have spread their resources wide, will stop at nothing to obtain the Palladium and once again try to forge a new dynasty ... this time, perhaps beyond a world war, if that's even possible.' Richard proceeded. 'We cannot leave this to chance again, my friends. As tragic as young Sami's suicide was it did thwart a greater evil ... perhaps she even knew this. We may not be so fortunate a second time.'

A cold pause fell as Mary managed to position herself within viewing distance of the semi-circle, crouching down out of sight. The five members, all with wooden staffs held in front of them, turned to one another with conflicting expressions.

'We can't, Richard. We just *can't*.' Nick spoke with fervour. 'None of us are murderers!' his agitation continued.

'Nick … we must consider the wider consequences here. We need time to locate Excalibur, and unless you can get through to Mack given his current state, we need all the cards in our hands, yes?' Richard stood firm.

'She's a *kid*, Richard. She doesn't know anything about all this. It's not her fight. Besides, do you think Luke is just going to let you kill her?' Nick moved aggressively towards his leader, prompting Gary and William to stand between them as the bickering broke out. Amongst the myriad of voices came another, directly inside Mary's head, as if someone stood by her side but she could not recognise them. 'It's not safe for you here. You must leave *now*.' it whispered gently. Mary felt a rush of pain and grief flood over her, flashes of Jenny's blood-soaked face, crushed by the twisted metal. Her skin began to burn, the voices in her head grew louder, too loud to cope with, she clamped her hands on her ears as she tried to settle them, only to have them become stronger.

Her actions caught Luke's eye as he rushed down the stairs to her side, skidding on the last step, releasing a few loose pebbles. Richard and the group spotted the two of them, their faces showing their horror when they realised what Mary might have heard.

'What the *hell* is going on?' Richard blurted angrily. 'Luke, I told you and your brother to wait upstairs!' Luke, now backed up by Adam, was about to make an apology when an ungodly noise rose from Mary – tongues none could decipher. Possibly Greek, possibly Latin, but raucous and variable like an off-key choir.

The walls and the very ground of the cave began to shake and rumble as the only sentence they understood reverberated from Mary's lips – *'You ... Lied ... To ... Me!'*

A cacophonous scream followed, before an explosion of incendiary orange flame engulfed the cave.

**Chapter 12**

**Boston, USA**

**24th November 2011 AD**

Elaine was expecting no further visitors today, despite the Thanksgiving celebrations. Having driven Luke and Mary over to the airport early that morning, she took time over a coffee to contemplate her call to her ex-husband. Her mind raced back to a short primary school lecture Richard had given so many years back, outlining his family's history back to the venerable Sir Ralph Allen, their involvement in the construction of the city of Bath alongside the Wood family of architects in the seventeenth and eighteenth centuries. Some children would be yawning at the first sight of a sepia photograph of the Bath Circus or Prior Park, whereas others would eagerly start to point out on the City map where they and their parents lived.

When Richard would shift into legends of knights and dragons, this of course grabbed every child's attention, with Elaine not exactly approving of Mr Allen's deviation from the curriculum, but nonetheless grateful for the entertainment. It was shortly after these lessons that they began dating. Luke was born before the wedding, something that perturbed both their families, but this spurred the wedding date forward before Adam followed. 'Our houses are truly united now,' Richard would joke upon Adam's birth and the completion of their nuptials, regular family life seeming a certainty.

She would listen to her husband for hours, some nights until daybreak, sometimes captivated, other times concerned. The hardest times were often in the presence of Richard's closest company. William of the Wood family, never married, apparently committed to his higher purpose, would convey a sense of disapproval over Elaine and Richard's decision to wed and start a family. Karen, although childless herself, would always be more supportive of the Allen family unit, and gladly took on the role of godmother for her boys when asked. She and Karen would fondly recall the birth of Nick's daughter Violet, the expression on Nick's face during his wife's labour, and the juxtaposed expression on their friend William's. It was heart-breaking to hear later that Nick's wife had succumbed to breast cancer before Violet turned ten.

The decision to move to Boston ahead of Luke's eighteenth was meant to be a positive alignment for all. Elaine's elder son would start university out there if he could, while Adam would soon turn of age, when he could forge his own path in life. While aware that Adam was potentially facing the most challenging period in young adulthood when she and Luke left, there was a quiet confidence that he would rise to it, he needed no guidance – least of all from Richard. That said, his loyalty to his father was unquestionable and she chose to distance herself, somewhat selfishly, so as not to be proven wrong. Needless to say she often incurred the wrath of Luke, and any challenges of her motives were outmanoeuvred with warnings not to contact his father or brother, safe in the knowledge Richard would likely be saying the same to Adam.

Elaine never contemplated Richard's world would somehow find her and Luke here, an ocean apart. She was never one to believe in fate, but recent incidents were close to making a believer out of her. For all her subterfuge and absent motherhood of recent years, she made the choice to intervene this time. Mary's health was fragile enough to tip the balance, to see history repeat itself. Her thoughts weighed heavy like a flagging racehorse, almost forcing her to open a bottle or two of red wine in an attempt to drown them out. But not this time, her actions were just, and she reassured herself that both her sons and Mary would be safe in England among learned hands.

A knock on the door broke her train of thought. It was still early, no post or deliveries expected – but always well-wishers from the close community. She frantically cleared any signs of alcohol from tables and work surfaces before opening the door to a man dressed neatly in a pressed suit. She did not recognise him, although he was as slick as a salesman.

'Mrs Allen? A happy Thanksgiving to you,' the gentleman politely began.

'It's Mrs Cole now, but thanks, and likewise to you, Sir,' she rebuffed. 'How may I help you?'

'Apologies for the intrusion, Mrs Cole. My name is Mr Mohammed Hussin, I work on the Harvard campus. I wondered if I could ask about your son?' he continued. Elaine's hair stood up on the back of her neck but she held a suitably composed demeanour.

'What would you like to know?' she enquired.

'Ah, you see I've heard he's a bit of a local mechanic? Many of the students have told us. A very good one I hear – I may even recommend him to the Dean if he keeps blaming his old motor as the reason for being late to committees,' Mr Hussin tried to lighten the mood. 'However, I'm sure you are aware of the tragic death of a student from the campus only recently ... Miss Jennifer Van Hansen? So very sad, a promising young talent.'

Elaine nodded without a word, ensuring she stood firmly between Mr Hussin and entry into her home. 'Yes, indeed. Tragic. I'm sorry, what has this got to do with my son?'

'We believe he, Luke, was close to the driver of the car that sadly saw the untimely death of Miss Van Hansen this summer. The driver in question being a Miss Mary Cassidy?' Mr Hussin continued, gently rubbing a thumb over his walking staff. 'Now, I appreciate this must be a very sensitive issue for you, Mrs Cole, but I'm sure you can understand, when the death of a student, and serious injury to another might have happened as a result of an unfortunate vehicle malfunction, a vehicle apparently serviced by a no doubt talented but unlicensed mechanic, parents and students begin to ask questions,' his voice became sterner.

Elaine remained silent. She wanted to ask the gentleman whether he'd tried to approach the local hospital, seek our Mr Cassidy, or whether he'd already tapped this source and traced it back. Either way, excuses not to answer the request, other than certification of identity or police warrants, were slipping from her rapidly.

'He's not here,' she eventually blurted out clumsily.

'I see. When will he be back?'

'Later, probably. Perhaps Miss Cassidy could help?' she sweated.

'Ah, I'm sure she could, Mrs Cole … or was it Mrs *Allen*? Apologies, it has been a long day,' came Mr Hussin's reply, growing in temerity. 'Sadly, we thought we'd heard Miss Mary Cassidy was taken to hospital only days ago, along with her father, but alas, when we arrived and asked staff we found that although Mr Cassidy remains critical but stable, Mary Cassidy had checked herself out. With assistance.'

Elaine's heart was now pounding, a tremor was visible through the half-open front door she held ajar. Taking a step back, she began to close the door in the face of her visitor while muttering 'I'm sorry I cannot help you.' – but Mr Hussin's staff blocked the corner.

'Do forgive my insistence Mrs Cole, but we really must know now,' his eyes flashed unnervingly.

'I really don't know what to tell you Mr Hussin. I suggest you wait and come back later.' Elaine said, panicking as she was still trying to get the door closed. With a final push it closed, and she immediately turned the lock before settling her back against it, regaining her breath. She leapt in fright as a silver blade pierced its way between the door and its frame, slicing through the lock. Both door and frame collapsed inwards with the force of Mr Hussin's kick, Elaine left cowering on her side in front of him.

'I'm afraid that really won't do, Mrs Cole. I have very impatient people awaiting my report you see,' he said, towering over her, the blade in his hand hovering inches above her head. 'Now, where is your son and Mary Cassidy?'

Perhaps it was the adrenaline of the action, or that brief but reassuring comfort that for all her misdeeds in the past and potential failure as a mother, she had this time done the right thing – Elaine was focused, not afraid to stare at her opponent directly. 'Whoever you are, whatever maniacal tribe you claim to follow, you won't endure.' knowing these words would be her trial and death sentence.

The blade swiped neatly above her breast, with a heavy sigh from Mr Hussin. He turned to face the winter air once more and reached into his pocket for his phone.

# Chapter 13

Glastonbury, England

25th November 2011 AD

Amidst the swirling clouds of dust and smoke, Luke tried to force himself to his feet, ears ringing and lungs gasping for clean air. The weight of his brother lay on his side, a shimmering blue circle shielding both of them from several large rocks that had fallen from all directions. Adam gave a heave with all the strength he could muster to free them both, steadying each other as they stood. They looked around frantically, shouting people's names in hope of reply. The dust slowly settled to reveal five fine beams of silvery white light casting through, the charred faces of Richard, William, Karen, Nick and Gary gradually being revealed. Luke briefly saw the five Red Dragon members with their swords on display, a stirring sight even under these most unfortunate of circumstances, but quickly they reverted to the more familiar wooden staffs, their magic having served its purpose of protection.

Karen and Gary were still lying on the ground from the force of the explosion. William and Nick rushed to their aid as Richard shouted over to his sons.

'Luke! Adam! Are you alright?'

'We're OK, Father.' Adam replied. Luke simply raised a hand in agreement, still out of breath.

'Where's Mary?' Karen coughed, leaning on William. Everyone scrambled through the rubble and called her name, but nothing.

'She can't have gone far.' William comforted them. Richard stood staring at the blocked entrance to the world outside. 'Unless she's on the other side of that,' he replied sternly.

Luke's strength was slowly returning, enough to challenge his father face-to-face. 'What the hell have you done? Stupid old man, with your myths and special gatherings. What right have you got, huh? To interfere with my and Mary's life?' his hands now gripped his father's collar as he spat out his words, Adam forcing his arm between the two to separate them.

'This isn't helping anyone, Luke.' Adam said, while wrestling him away from Richard. 'We need to get out of here and go find her, *now*.' Gary and Nick were already working on moving the boulders from the stairway.

'If she is bloody alive!' Luke shouted.

'She will be, son.' Richard said calmly, catching Luke off guard. 'I don't suppose during your time together Mary has regularly displayed such actions? Why do you think your mother contacted me?' he asked. Luke remained silent while turning his back to Richard, hands on the back of his head, still fuming.

'She is a messenger, a reincarnation if you will, of Athena. Brought forth out of tragedy through the loss of a loved one, a dear friend, now consumed with grief and pain,' he continued, head lowered.

'Save it for the kids, Dad. I know the story!' Luke snapped, despite knowing deep inside that everything he said had some sense of twisted logic. Richard stood quietly in thought as Nick and Gary enthusiastically moved away rock after rock, beginning to make some headway. 'I have, however, failed you all, I fear.' His words paused all action.

'This wasn't your fault, Richard.' Karen reassured. 'You've experienced this very thing ... with Elaine, remember? You had to act, we all had to,' her hand now holding his.

'I did. But in acting I have become predictable I fear,' he said.

'I don't understand,' Gary said, wiping dust from his face.

'Lady Morgan and the White Dragon would likely have known our protocol. Us gathering here under the Glastonbury Thorn as in times past for formal council. Lady Morgan with the Necklace of Harmonia would no doubt have picked up on an energy surge like that ... maybe even when Mary first fell into it in Boston ... who knows? But bringing her and Luke here, bringing you *all* here, might well have sealed out fate.' Richard spoke remorsefully.

Luke gave a disapproving snort, and was quickly shunned by Adam. 'She is still alive, Father, you said so yourself. Even if

Lady Morgan and Sir Lawrence have her, we owe it to Mary to try and save her,' Adam announced. A look of appreciation came across Karen's face as she patted Richard on the shoulder.

'We're *through*.' Nick echoed, as he haphazardly stumped over the remaining rocks on the stairway. Luke impatiently followed, still calling out Mary's name.

✛      ✛      ✛

Out in the evening light Mary sat alone on the kerb of the road, shivering in the drizzle while still holding Luke's jacket tightly round her. A few curious faces appeared at the windows of the homes opposite the Chalice Well, wondering what all the commotion was as two black Land Rovers pulled up alongside its entrance. High heels clicked on the cobbled pavement towards Mary, an umbrella appeared over her head offering shelter.

'Are you alright, my Dear?' came a soothing voice. Mary glanced up at the plain, gray raincoat above her, silver hair framing smooth but slightly aged skin, pale eyes welcoming. She knelt when Mary was unable to reply, arm stretched around her shoulders. 'You appear to be quite special … Miss Cassidy isn't it?' the lady continued, now piquing Mary's interest.

'You ... you know who I am?' Mary whimpered.

'Oh yes, I believe I do. And I am so sorry for your loss, the sudden departure of a close friend must be so bitter to taste. Especially when you feel all the blame lies upon you.'

Mary was stunned to silence at the lady's words. How was this possible? Was this a friend of Luke's? Of Richard or the Allen family? A part of her didn't seem to care, if only to hear such a reassuring and soothing voice tackle all her inner fears with such frankness.

'I think I may be able to help you,' the lady said. 'You must have so many questions, all yet to be answered. Let me provide you with those answers.' She stood offering her hand, and Mary accepted, noticing the fine red jewel glowing around her neck despite the lack of any natural light to make it sparkle.

'How do you know me?' Mary asked gingerly as she followed the lady to the first Land Rover.

'Oh, my dear, I've known of you a very long time. Please come, and all will be explained.'

Mary slid into the back seat as the lady took her place alongside her, ordering the driver to leave. The vehicles pulled away swiftly just as Luke and Adam burst through the Chalice Well entrance onto the main road. Luke continued to shout Mary's name as he and Adam split in opposite directions, scouting down the smaller side streets.

They both returned to the entrance, joining Richard and the wider group, frustrated and breathless. 'She's nowhere,' Adam reported.

Richard inspected the fresh tread marks in the mud by the kerb, William looking over his shoulder. 'Someone left in a hurry.' he claimed. Richard uh-huhed in agreement.

'Go back to Bath, all of you.' Richard ordered.

'Are you kidding me?' Luke protested. 'What do you want us to do exactly? Call the police?'

'Yes. That's exactly what I want you to do. Nick – can you get everyone in your car?' Richard replied. Nick huffed a yes.

'Good. I'll meet you back there.'

'Where are you going?' William asked with concern.

'Please trust me on this, friend. Get them back to The Bear. I'll join you shortly.' Richard insisted. William gave a doubtful look but obeyed the order as Richard jumped in his car and headed off in the same direction as the Land Rovers.

'Where's he going?' Karen asked. William gave no response, but held her tightly and urged her to get into Nick's car. Before he had a chance to herd Adam and Luke, Luke had darted across the road towards an unlocked motorbike, putting his rougher skills to use in hotwiring it, revving its engine several times.

'Luke? What are you doing?' Adam yelled, dodging traffic to join him on his side of the road.

'You can sit here and take orders from Dad if you want. I'm going after Mary!' Luke growled. Adam didn't have time to argue but he wasn't going to leave his brother. Gripping his waist, he straddled the back of the bike. 'Please remember ... you drive on the *left* here.' Adam mentioned casually as Luke spun the back wheel with urgency.

'What is it with that family?' Gary cursed.

Chapter 14

London, England

25th November 2011 AD

Hot tea was served in fine china cups, almost too fragile to hold by the handle. Mary had sat alone for no more than an hour in the oak panelled room, occasionally moving to the windows to take in the city skyline and renowned sites of the capital. She could just make out the dome of St Paul's Cathedral and the beige columns of the Palace of Westminster. Big Ben chimed regularly every fifteen minutes. The only other sounds besides this and the roaring traffic outside were the whispers coming from behind the door, snippets of bickering and movement orders barked to guard all entrances and exits.

Mary's mind was still churning – why was all this happening? Were Luke and his family alright? Was she alright? The tea was bitter despite two lumps of sugar, and she dare not ask for coffee. The main door creaked open and the lady who had ushered her into the Land Rover earlier spoke to her warmly.

'I'm so sorry my Dear. All a touch hectic here today, I'm sure you can imagine. Do you like the tea?' the lady asked. Mary nodded politely, hiding her dislike. 'Now, I'm sure you must have so many questions, I do too. So, why don't we go about trying to answer them together?'

Mary scanned the room uncomfortably before making eye contact with the lady again. 'Please don't be afraid, Mary. Why don't I start? I'm Morgan Worthington. I'm … well, fairly old, lived in England most of my life. Met my husband here in London, this very room in fact.' She gave a subtle grin, reaching for a china cup. 'He's a wonderful man.' she continued while pouring tea. 'So ambitious, nothing appeared to be a challenge for him. And so articulate! Never known a mind like Lawrence's.' she gushed, taking a sip.

'But, alas. I always felt something was missing, like I was being held back. Do you know such a feeling, Mary? Sure you do. Such an intelligent young woman. You must have big dreams?' Lady Morgan probed.

Mary ran her fingers round the rim of her cup, trying to come up with a response. 'I certainly do have dreams.' She spoke softly.

'Tell me about them.' Lady Morgan instructed. Mary hesitated for a moment before answering.

'I know what you mean. About … being held back and all. I never considered it recently but since … well, since this summer.'

'You lost someone, didn't you?'

'Yes.'

'And it changed your perspective on things, right?'

Mary felt the burning across her skin once more, and she trembled so hard that her teacup rattled on its saucer and she had to set it down. Lady Morgan studied her briefly before reaching both arms out across the table to hold Mary's hands. The moment they touched, Lady Morgan's jaw clenched, eyes screwed shut, as if suddenly in pain. Mary quickly withdrew and stood.

'I'm sorry. I … I can't explain any of this right now.' Mary began to break down.

'No. No, Mary you don't need to apologise. I overstepped the mark; the fault is mine.' Lady Morgan replied, rushing to her side. 'Losing someone you love can stir feelings we never knew were hidden. It can make us question what our true purpose in life is. What is it that we really want? What is it that we're missing? And how do we go about righting so many wrongs?'

Mary suddenly felt safe, she did not know why. But after all the hours spent with specialists and grievance counsellors over the past weeks not one had encapsulated or dared address her own immediate future – they were only interested in dealing with her past. A past she so desperately wanted to leave behind.

'Did you lose someone?' Mary asked.

'I did. In fact, I've lost a great many people over my life,' Lady Morgan sombrely replied. 'But I realised one day that you must always look forward, never back. What's done is done. You learn from it and move on.' She guided Mary back to her chair.

'Tell me, Mary, if I were to ask you right now, what is it that you want?' she questioned, still holding her hands. Mary pondered before answering.

'I want this all to stop. The guilt, the pain I'm causing,' she felt the burning rise within her once again. 'I want to see Jenny.' she cried. The table shuddered, prompting Lady Morgan to hold Mary's hands tighter, closing her eyes and concentrating.

'Jenny. Is that whom you've lost?' she whispered. Mary whispered a yes. 'To the sea? No. The ocean?' Lady Morgan persisted, as if in a trance, chin now resting on Mary's shoulder.

'No. It was ...' Mary tried to explain through her tears.

'An accident. A tragic accident? Of course ... as it was foretold in legend.' Lady Morgan continued her musings. Mary was not following, but aware the grip on her hands had tightened.

'There was a wreck. A twisted metal shell,' Lady Morgan went on. Mary could only think she was referring to the car accident that claimed Jenny's life. She tried to explain the details, but Lady Morgan wasn't listening anymore. Something about a sunken ship, a warship, many years ago – Mary couldn't place any of it. All she knew was her feeling of reassurance was beginning to ebb away.

There was a knock on the door which distracted both. An official-looking gentleman entered and bowed his head. 'Do excuse me, Lady Morgan, we have a situation down in the lobby,' he said firmly. At his insistence, Lady Morgan followed him out of the room.

Mary rubbed the tears from her eyes, then headed for the window, her attention caught by the flicker of blue lights and the sound of sirens. She spotted what looked like Richard, confronted by police officers as he protested he needed to gain entry. At first, the officers appeared successful in their approach as Richard turned away in submission, only to swiftly turn his staff upon both, knocking them down onto the steps. He shot inside.

'Lawrence!' came Richard's booming voice through the lobby. Two on-site security guards unsuccessfully tried to restrain his tall frame as Tristan trotted down one side of the balcony stairs.

'I'm afraid Sir Lawrence is not here, Mr Allen. Might I suggest making an appointment?' he quipped.

'Save it Tristan. *Where is he*? And where's his she-devil of a mistress?' Richard barked in reply, shaking off the two guards.

'Now Mr Allen, I really don't believe we need to cause a scene here. You must know more police will be on their way,' Tristan calmly responded, bringing out his own staff. Richard took a step back.

'Fine. You want to settle this? Then let's settle this!' Richard grimaced, grasping his staff with both hands, ready to strike.

'Gentlemen. That won't be necessary.' came the familiar hiss of Lady Morgan from the balcony. Richard and Tristan stood down, Richard's sights now set firmly on the ashen figure above him. 'Mr Baker. Please can you call the local forces and tell them there is no need for alarm ... then join the others,' she ordered.

'But, my Lady ...?' Tristan stood stunned.

'Now, please,' she confirmed. No more was needed. 'Mr Allen, why don't you join us?'

Richard watched Tristan turn and leave before tentatively climbing the stairs, glancing over both sides, expecting an ambush. 'It's quite safe, I promise you,' Lady Morgan assured him.

'A promise? From you?' Richard growled.

'Come now, Richard. You know I am many things, but I am no liar,' she replied.

Mary had managed to make her way through to the main corridor, curiosity getting the better of her. If Richard was here, was Luke far behind? She had to know. She tiptoed past the marble columns that dominated the hallway, taking shelter behind one as Richard approached her host.

'Where is the girl, Morgan?' Richard demanded.

'The "girl"? Why Richard, you and I both know she's far more than that.' Lady Morgan said. 'Such a treasure of a mind, a gift.

Wouldn't you agree?' She brought a hand to Richard's cheek, curling a finger round his ear affectionately. Richard seized her wrist with temper.

'No games, Morgan. *Where is she*?' he cursed. Lady Morgan turned her head in Mary's direction, as if she were standing in plain sight. 'Please come out, my dear,' she requested. Mary instinctively twisted away, further behind the column, holding her breath. 'It's quite alright, Mary. Please trust me,' Lady Morgan insisted.

Mary slowly made herself known to the two of them, edging closer in short steps. Lady Morgan took a place by her side. 'My dear Mary. I believe this man knows you? Do you know him?'

Mary nodded in agreement, staring directly at Richard.

'Perhaps you could tell me how you know him?' Lady Morgan asked, unsettling Richard.

'He's ... he's the father of Luke. My boyfriend,' Mary stuttered.

'Your *boyfriend*? How ... chivalrous. Wouldn't you agree, Richard?' Lady Morgan said sweetly. 'He and his father here must care a great deal about you. To come all this way, just for you.'

'Morgan!' Richard warned.

'But yet, when I found you, you were all alone, so desperate, so ... so *weak*.' Lady Morgan teased. 'Why, whatever happened to leave you in such a state of despair?'

'Morgan, *enough*.' Richard boomed again, staff held defensively. The damage had, however, been done. Mary's eyes flashed vivid red and orange, smouldering embers, her fists clenched, skin smouldering. *'You ... Lied ... To ... Me!'*

Richard acted without hesitation, swinging his staff round, broadly aiming for Mary's throat. The revealed blade shone brilliantly, only to stop inexplicably inches from its target. He gritted his teeth, straining, so eager to finish the blow, but Mary just stood there stubbornly, as if impenetrable. His arms shook with a counter force that could not be seen, only felt – bending his sword back upon itself before shattering it into pieces. He staggered back in shock.

His body began to freeze, every muscle under strain, paralysed. He could feel the immense heat generated by Mary and seemingly focused directly upon him. Air was being burnt from his lungs; his blood was close to boiling as he started to succumb to the pain. Mary remained undaunted, almost sadistically pleased with the thought of subduing her would-be assailant. Lady Morgan stood patiently, sensing her effortless victory. Only a familiar voice bellowing her name was enough to break Mary's compulsion.

'Min ... Min! It's me, Babe!' Luke shouted from the lobby. 'Please ... whatever you're doing, please stop!' he pleaded.

Mary's eyes began to well up at the sight of Luke, and whatever force had captivated her lifted. Her focused anger and pain gave way to the familiar confusion and bewilderment as

Richard fell to the lobby floor unconscious. Adam barged passed his brother, rushing to his father's aid.

'Min. I know you're upset; we all are. Trust me ... we'll figure it out together,' Luke begged. Mary tried to force a smile to welcome his support, only to be conflicted by the hiss of Lady Morgan once more.

'You think they care about you? You think that they know you? Look what they tried to do ... what *he* tried to do. Their family. You're not one of them,' she whispered without inflection. Luke's saddened expression and outstretched hand confused Mary, she glanced down to see Adam cradling Richard, desperately trying to bring him round as the screeching sound of tyres echoed from outside.

'Luke. We've got to go ... *now.*' Adam commanded, trying to pull Richard to his feet.

'A wise choice, Master Allen,' Lady Morgan said, while turning Mary away and swiftly leading her back down the hallway.

'Min. Min, *wait.*' Luke gave chase, only to be cut off by two towering hooded figures appearing from either side. Not police, not military, but anonymously dressed in black, and square in stature. He threw a punch at one of the balaclava-covered faces which barely registered before he was pinned roughly to the wall.

'Luke!' Adam shouted, laying his father back down only to note more of Lady Morgan's reinforcements approaching the main entrance to the lobby. 'Oh great.' he quipped. Standing sentry, Adam waited for the first of the figures to crash through the glass door before deflecting a loose fist and countering with one of his own – his making contact. Another figure barrelled through furiously into the affray, granting Adam the chance to catch his wrist and flip him over onto the small of his back. The third was put down by a simple kick to the chest.

'Luke!' Adam shouted again as he watched his brother grapple with the two figures on the balcony. The glint of a knife appeared in the hands of one, resisted by Luke as he struck a knee into the groin of the other. Adam charged up the stairs and threw himself on the back of the shank-wielding figure, digging a thumb deep into his windpipe, forcing him to stumble back choking, dropping his weapon. Luke seized a vase from a side table and instructed his brother to duck as he smashed it hard over the figure's head.

'Thanks. Now can we go?' Adam wheezed.

'But what about Mary?' Luke gasped, bowed over catching his own breath.

'We'll figure it out. We've got to get Dad out of here.' Adam insisted, watching what he thought to be the last of the hooded figures come back on his feet still holding his groin. Only he wasn't the last, as more veiled figures appeared from down the hall, all now armed with more than just knives, too many to fend off. Adam pushed Luke behind him and readied his shield. They might be able to run, jump through a window, bolt for another room – but each option seemed to expire as soon as it was formed in Adam's mind. He simply stood in defence of his brother, unsure for how long, as guns clicked and loaded. Then a flash of blue light shot across both their heads and landed amongst their attackers, tossing them into the marble columns and hallway walls like paper caught in the wind.

Adam and Luke looked at one another in silence, then turned back down towards the lobby to see the ash-blonde hair and ginger stubble, familiar only to Adam.

'Can't seem to leave you alone for more than five minutes can I, me Lad?' Iain Donnelly smiled.

## Chapter 15

Tintagel, England

26th November 2011 AD

Sir Lawrence had spent much of his life contemplating his pedigree. Ancestral lineage through the Knights of Sir Lancelot, founding member of the White Dragon, and fealty to Morgan Le Fay. A shaper of worlds, but also a destroyer, never drawn into the causalities of good vs. evil, right vs. wrong – only balance. His thoughts would often turn to his counterparts, the Red Dragon, headed by the Knights of Sir Galahad, equal loyalty to King Arthur and the perceived protection of Excalibur. They themselves embodied the balance so needed in nature, he could hardly bring himself to call them enemies.

But what could even a legendary sword bring to this fight? When a sacred statue imbued with the power of a Greek goddess was capable of forging empires at its holder's will, and a necklace crafted in counterpart was destined to follow and destroy in a pattern of war and greed. Did this not epitomise a pure circle of life? Was his faction all that needed to be or needed to exist? It was a debate long held amongst those closest to him over many a century, and one not likely to be resolved any time soon.

It was still a surprise to have Lady Morgan request a gathering upon the very site of King Arthur's birth. Whether this was done as a statement or out of necessity was never questioned. Lady Morgan had summoned the White Dragon Knights to meet her and Tristan among the ruins of the castle, without formality. All were fully prepared to witness her gamble pay off, the clarification of decades' worth of fragmented visions finally amalgamated in a candid unveiling of the Palladium – all through the forces of Athena's reincarnation, a young woman from Boston, USA.

'She mentioned the ocean?' Colonel Thorpe commented as he stood rigidly by Sir Lawrence's side, overlooking the crisp Cornish coastline bathed in fading evening light. Despite Lady Morgan's nonchalance, Sir Lawrence was not taking any chances with Richard and the Red Dragon now so deeply embroiled, and had the colonel bring his own personal armed guard.

'She did. But I doubt we'll have need for a submarine just yet,' Sir Lawrence noted, checking his watch.

'What about Mohammed?' the colonel asked.

'Mr Hussin will not be joining us. While I have every faith in my wife, my head is telling me to keep some resources at a distance. He will return to Jordan.' Stephen gave approval while looking over his shoulder to glimpse the headlights of the Land Rover descending the winding coast path – she was here.

## Chapter 16

**Bath, England**

**26th November 2011 AD**

Iain took three long gulps of lager before wiping the slight dribble from his chin. 'It's like I've been tellin' ya. Sacred Band members have been watching the works of the White Dragon for years now, not always asking your approval like.' he stated.

William and Karen sat opposite him pensively, Gary simply scratching his head while Nick cleared away the two empty glasses finished off by his Irish guest. The Bear had been closed on short notice upon Richard's return, at Adam's insistence, as Violet tended to him upstairs.

Luke leant his head back against the brickwork of the fireplace in frustration. 'Look, this isn't getting us anywhere is it? Mary's still out there and we don't have a clue where this cult has taken her or what it plans to do.' he spat.

'I don't think it's going to be like the Wicker Man, Luke.' Adam reassured. Luke did not quite get the reference, or his brother's attempt at humour. 'Whatever Mary is … or has … it's fair to say Lady Morgan and the White Dragon need her alive.'

'We know what she is,' William interjected. 'We just didn't know whether to believe your father. Luke – Elaine told you about the case in Birmingham all those years ago, yes?'

'Yeah. Sounded farfetched then.' Luke admitted.

'Indeed. Was there anything else she shared? Anything Richard might have noted about ritual or protocol?' William enquired. Luke shook his head.

Adam pondered for a moment. 'Have you actually spoken to her since you arrived here?' he said coldly. Luke gave another shake of the head, this time the colour draining from his face. He dived into his pocket for his mobile and frantically swiped through his contacts.

'Was there anything else you've picked up on about Lady Morgan and the White Dragon?' Gary continued to quiz Iain.

'Other than the occasional reference to international affairs – all quite alarming like – no, sadly not,' he confessed. 'I did though overhear word of an operation ... operation *Dumnonii* -- shortly before they left for Glastonbury. Mean anything to you lot?' he asked.

All cast blank looks at one another before a gravelly voice came from behind -- 'Cornwall.' Richard staggered down the steps, still weary-eyed and sore, Violet standing attentively at his side. 'Tintagel most likely.' He took a seat next to Karen.

'Richard, you really shouldn't be out of bed,' she fussed. He waved his hand in dismissal.

'Mr Donnelly, I'm sure I need not stress to you the importance of ....' Richard lectured before Iain cut in.

'I know, I know. I didn't undertake this task without knowing its reason. Your young lad and I know what's at stake,' he stated, giving Adam a warm smile, almost causing a blush across his cheeks. 'I'm guessing we also don't have much time?'

'No, we do not.' Richard stood up. 'Friends, I must ask you to take a stand with me. I know I put you in danger, all of you – and my actions have been reckless. I didn't want any of you to get hurt, or fall foul of any false prophesies, but I know I cannot do this without you.' He turned to Adam, his son looking straight back at him, before turning to the floor.

All stood in acknowledgement, holding staffs by their sides, the moment of solidarity broken by Luke bursting through the pub door – Elaine wasn't answering. A line of sweat formed across Richard's bruised brow ... time was indeed very short.

**Chapter 17**

**Tintagel, England**

**26th November 2011 AD**

The saline breeze was enough to refresh Mary as she made her way across the narrow wooden bridge to the castle ruins. She had been reminded of the beauty of the Cornish coast by both Luke and his mother, putting it high on her list of places to visit when visiting Britain, but these were not the circumstances she envisaged.

The breeze turned into muscled blasts of chilling sea air as she and Lady Morgan reached the summit, Tristan not far behind. Armed soldiers punctuated the landmark, some with their faces covered, others fully exposed – enough to dry the mouth of their hostage. Her thoughts turned to Luke once more, thoughts tinged with a potent mix of venom and desire as she was beckoned forward to the cliff edge by Lady Morgan. She would give anything to have him here now, just to hear his voice to drown out the incessant noise of Jenny's screams ringing in her head.

Lady Morgan took Mary's hands in hers once more, Sir Lawrence and others a suitable distance back. She gave an impassive look to all before focusing back on Mary.

'Isn't it beautiful? I would come here so often as a child, wonder what lay beyond. Looked a little different back then of course,' Lady Morgan said. Mary was still desperately assessing the situation, taking a dizzying look down on the jagged rocks below, the crash of the waves casting spray. Was she about to be pushed off to her death? Was this an ultimatum or threat of some kind? She made her unease known.

'Are you going to kill me?' she meekly asked.

Lady Morgan looked shocked. 'Kill you? Oh, my dear child, not at all. How could anyone take the life of someone so precious, so … important. A living goddess.'

If Mary wasn't confused before, she certainly was now. A living goddess? Her perplexed expression said it all.

'Let me explain …' Lady Morgan continued, with an arm around Mary's waist. 'What's happening to you is no accident, it has been foretold. I tried to see it but couldn't fathom it. It was all unclear, like a mist in my mind. Then, one day a spark … a candle lit in the bleak wilderness, guiding me back to its resting place. It's happened before, teasing me almost, only to flicker out just when I got close, but not this time. Not with you.'

'I'm a *goddess*?' Mary shuddered.

'Yes, at least the voice of one, here in our world. So lost, so alone. Born out of pain and tribulation,' Lady Morgan continued.

Mary started to close her eyes, a sense of calm came upon her like an instant tonic, the voices became clearer – Jenny, Luke, Elaine, her father – now distinguishable from one another, no longer in conflict. She gripped Lady Morgan's arms with eagerness, yearning for more words to soothe her suffering.

'That's it … close your eyes. Keep them closed,' Lady Morgan urged. 'Think of Jenny … what you felt, what you still feel now.'

The burning came once more through Mary's body, only this time, in controlled bursts, non-threatening. She felt the pulse of the sea, but far further than the coast. A focal point deep below the surface – a metal wreck, a ship. It had known love, but also pain. She opened her eyes briefly, only to see Lady Morgan had her eyes closed tightly in a trance – she could feel everything Mary herself was experiencing, she was a mirror of both the emotional and the physical. The skin was burning, almost burst into flame, the grass beneath their feet scorched and withered, the sea itself churning.

'I see it.' Lady Morgan proclaimed. *'I … See … It!'*

# Chapter 18

Tintagel, England

26th November 2011 AD

Luke groped his hands around the back seat of William's car. 'Please tell me you've got more than just screen wash and a copy of the *Bath Chronicle* as weapons here?' he blurted. Having witnessed back in London what must have been a fraction of the firepower Lady Morgan and Sir Lawrence had at their disposal, there was a certainty that any confrontation now would be at full tilt.

Richard was tapping numbers on his mobile, trying to reach Elaine – still no answer. Each failed attempt saw a rise in his agitation. 'Keep trying,' William urged, ignoring all speed limits and occasionally glancing back to ensure Karen and Gary were keeping up.

Adam and Iain sat quietly either side of Luke, tutting at his squirming as he continued to rummage around for anything remotely useful as a weapon. 'Luke – I know you're scared, we all are, but trust me when I say there's nothing in this Vauxhall that is going to bring down Lady Morgan and any other White Dragon knight.' he said dismissively.

'Aside from the people in it.' smiled Iain.

'Perhaps.' Adam noted.

Iain drummed his nails on the window in distraction. 'So...you've lived in the States?' he turned to Luke. 'Still do,' Luke corrected in reply.

'Ah, never been there m'self. Kept meaning to go see a cousin out there in Maine but couldn't get around to it.'

'I can imagine the whole double-agent business does keep you busy, yes,' Luke retorted, receiving an elbow in the ribs from Adam. Iain appeared to brush the remark off.

'How did you get involved with all this? The White Dragon I mean?' Adam asked. 'They're not exactly open to new members.'

Iain chuckled. 'True that. And nor are your family either, or your Red counterparts? But let's be honest lad, as members of the Sacred Band we don't always get to pick sides, do we? We've had our own legacy going back far longer than King Arthur's lot … it's only wise to keep an eye on both, wouldn't you say?'

Adam raised an eyebrow, not quite sure how to respond. He'd always loyally believed that his father's side, the Red Dragon, and its enlisting of Sacred Band members across the world, was in the name of justice and protection – why else would his people choose to align themselves with them for so very long? The notion that both Red and White stemmed from the same collective linage of the Round Table, at inception working together at the request of the great King of Britain, never really crossed his mind. Perhaps the adage of two sides, same coin was indeed appropriate here. He pushed these thoughts back – 'I think I know which side I need to be on. I'm sure you do too,' he defended.

'I do lad, I do.' Iain replied, humour dissipating.

'I'm sorry ... would you like me to switch seats?' Luke bristled at Adam in frustration – only to be interrupted by Richard from the front. 'Luke. *Enough*. I still can't get your mother ... I'll have Nick and Violet continue to try from The Bear.' The quaver in his voice was enough to dampen Luke's temper. Richard had sensibly decided to leave Nick in Bath, if only to protect Violet ... but also mindful that what they were about to engage with might require considerable sacrifice. Not all the pieces on the board needed to be manoeuvred just yet.

The mobile rang, and Richard answered hastily, expecting Elaine, only to hear Karen's voice. 'You guys seeing this?' she asked. William pointed at the sombre clouds appearing over the village of Tintagel, broken by strange bursts of amber lightning and claps of thunder. The sea was dancing unusually, the gusts of wind growing ever stronger.

'Whatever's happening over there, we need to move fast.' William said, pulling his car sharply into the nearest layby, Karen and Gary swift to follow.

✢   ✢   ✢

A grassy knoll just to the south of the castle island provided a good vantage point. Karen adjusted her binoculars the best she could. She spotted Lady Morgan, Mary by her side, other figures less well defined.

'What's going on?' Luke said impatiently.

'Lady Morgan has Mary ... I can't make it out though. It's like a ritual of some sorts, Mary's giving off some sort of energy, a fire?' Karen described, before turning to Richard.

'What the hell does that mean?' Luke continued to fuss, getting ready to rise to his feet as Richard pulled him back down.

'You don't understand, Luke. Mary ... she has something within her, a power – that's what Lady Morgan and the White Dragon want, not Mary herself. But that power is unstable, fuelled with rage and pain. If we simply strike, we may not survive ... any of us.' he said.

Luke was still dismissive, knowing that Mary, for all her faults, all his wrongdoings, would never want to harm anyone – but the thought of causing her more anguish was enough to make him hold back for now. Gary had been focusing on the mushroom clouds swelling above, and how the lightning appeared to be striking further out to sea, as if illuminating something. He caught Richard's eye and pointed farther out beyond the coast. Richard pondered before his eyes widened.

The Palladium, it was out there, and Mary was guiding Lady Morgan right to it. 'We need to move. *Now*.' he commanded.

'Might want to rethink that, friend,' Iain uttered, casting a nod towards the heavy-duty vehicles lined up by the coastal path. Whether they could see it or not, they were most certainly outnumbered.

It was now Richard that was growing impatient, knowing that any moment now his adversaries would have their hands on the statue, drawn deep from the ocean with Mary as the magnet. The numbers against them almost seemed irrelevant. 'Let us draw them away at least. Give you and your knights a chance?' Iain insisted.

'Us?' Richard enquired, only to have Iain place a hand on Adam's shoulder. Richard froze for a moment at the idea of his son as bait, but Adam's own look of reassurance left him with little choice. 'Very well,' he agreed.

'Get Luke in closer,' Adam said, holding his father's arm as the group parted. 'He might be the only one that can reach Mary now.' Suddenly the reality of having both his sons in the firing line tore him between what was parentally moral and that which was necessary. There would come a time when he would need to explain every action he took to his children, and maybe he wouldn't get to choose when that time was or how long he would be granted to confess – if a look of pride was all he was permitted, that would have to suffice.

## Chapter 19

**Tintagel, England**

**26th November 2011 AD.**

'What do you think is out there?' William asked, as he and Karen took shelter just under a rocky overhang directly beneath the main castle structure. Karen struggled for footing, leaning back heavily while trying not to look at the churning waves below.

'Sami, the young girl from Birmingham Richard spoke of. She drowned in a canal, suicide. But I remember him discussing visions she had shortly before that. Visions of the ocean, trapped inside, struggling for breath.' Karen said, still trying to anchor herself. 'It was as if her visions were memories, not of her own making but brought about by the grief of loss.'

'You think the Palladium is trapped in the ocean?' William asked.

'Makes sense. Think about it … what if the Palladium didn't remain in Nazi Germany? What if their empire needed to conquer more than just land, also sea? What if that was pivotal to your success? A battle in the Atlantic, a strategically vital move from Hitler in the subjugation of Britain – no convoys, no food, no real bloodshed either.'

'You think the Nazis placed the Palladium aboard a ship?'

'Not just any ship. Their flagship. The vanguard of the entire German Navy.'

'*Bismarck*?'

Karen looked up at the increasingly tumultuous skies. 'Not the easiest of places to go and search if you've lost a statue only a foot high,' she continued. 'Especially if Lady Morgan had become so accustomed to knowing its whereabouts for many a century.'

William pulled a pensive frown before noting the fate of the Knights of Lamorak, and one of the six missing White Dragon members. A bloodline that had died out around about the time of the Second World War, so many sons and daughters lost. Could it be this was his fate?

Richard and Gary had made their way to the other side of the island mound, Luke proving surprisingly nimble as he scrabbled towards a ruined wall just below two guards. He could see Mary, serene while fire and lightning engulfed her, with Lady Morgan still holding her tightly, the bright red glow of Lady Morgan's necklace separating the two. There was no struggle, almost a willingness from Mary towards the embrace, as if a balm for the wounds she bore. Whatever was surging through her appeared to be lifting, drawn out, increasing Richard and William's own discomfort at the situation.

Lady Morgan released an arm and stretched it out towards the sea, momentarily stalling the intense lightning storm above them. Far in the distance a dim beacon of light pulsed, faint at first but gradually increasing in luminosity. Sir Lawrence crept forward in anticipation, his own breath breaking the sudden eerie silence that had fallen. A silence replaced by the explosion immediately behind them as one of the Land Rovers went up in smoke. Guards spun around in distraction, with Colonel Thorpe barking orders to investigate.

✢     ✢     ✢

'Think they noticed that?' Iain smirked, clearing his throat a little from the heavy smoke swirling round the burning vehicle which had collapsed on its wheels. Adam shook the shock from his face, thinking there might have been more subtle means of distraction than plunging a blue flaming spear deep into the fuel tank, despite how impressive and apparently effective it proved to be. The thunder of feet grew louder as guards hurried back to the coastal path, guns loaded. 'Might I suggest we find cover?' Adam said sarcastically, as a few stray bullets flew past.

Sir Lawrence remained rooted, instructing Tristan to do the same – any such shenanigans from the Red Dragon were not going to spoil his prize, that much was clear. Staffs were raised in anticipation of attack, he and Tristan standing back to back monitoring all sides.

'We must do it *now*.' William muttered to Karen. 'What's Richard waiting for?'

Karen desperately looked to the far side of the ruins for any signal from Richard or Gary, but nothing. Maybe he was waiting? Waiting to see if the Palladium does indeed find its way back to Lady Morgan, then strike to seize it from the White Dragon once and for all. She touched William's hand for patience.

Lady Morgan for the first time began to show excitement, a tremble of anticipation as she gripped Mary tighter, causing Mary to wince and struggle. 'Yes ... Yes! Come to me. Come home!' her words carried on the breeze. Mary's discomfort prodded Luke into action. He rose to his feet while clumsily kicking over some loose stone fragments as Gary pulled him back. The commotion was enough to draw the attention of a derisive Sir Lawrence.

'What are you hiding for, Richard?' he bellowed. 'This is what you wanted, wasn't it? To see the Palladium after all these centuries? Now you *can*. And all the Red Dragon can witness its one and true purpose ... a balanced world. A *better world*.'

Unbeknown to Gary or Luke, Richard had made his move, scrambling to the far side of a ruined wall cast in shadow, close enough to finally see Karen and William and give a signal to engage with the scattered guards up top. He emerged from his hiding spot; hands held high in submission.

'Don't do this, Lawrence. You'll kill the girl.' he pleaded.

'What do you care?' Sir Lawrence snorted. 'I'm informed that just moments earlier this would be doing you a favour?' The tip of his staff was aimed directly at Richard. 'My dear fellow … no staff of your own? What happened?' he mocked.

'I tried to play God,' Richard replied, expressionless.

Sir Lawrence bit his bottom lip in curiosity as Tristan urged him to finish the job and dispatch the rival once and for all. But Richard's capitulation was too easy, too sincere, enough to keep Sir Lawrence alert but reserved. He lowered his staff for a moment – 'Well. Some of us are not meant to be Mr Allen,' he casually replied.

'Indeed, you are right, Lawrence,' came a resolved response as two guards fell from the castle walls to the ground, replaced by the bright swords of William and Karen. Tristan yelled in alarm as Gary appeared, leaping from behind the wall and swinging his blade fiercely, Tristan ducking just in time and staging a counterattack, sparks of white spraying as their blades collided.

'So be it,' Sir Lawrence concluded as he unlocked the end of his ornate staff to reveal another within, both instantly transforming into two separate blades with which he skilfully diced the air around Richard, who frantically dodged and dived, until Karen and William engaged to repel the attack. A route had been cleared to reach Mary and Lady Morgan, something of which Luke had also taken advantage.

✢     ✢     ✢

The circle of orange flame was still tightly around Mary and Lady Morgan, reaching waist height as Luke approached. The heat was intense, smoke rising from the scorched earth beneath his feet as the energy emanating from the two pulsed stronger. He waved a palm in front of himself in an attempt to force his way through, but Lady Morgan spotted his action and flicked her finger to bring the wall of fire high above his head, repelling him. Richard caught him under the arm to break his fall. 'Stay here!' he commanded.

Richard moved as close as he could to the flames, coat pressed over his mouth to keep out the smoke, muffling his speech.

'Morgan.' he coughed. 'Stop this. This is not her fight!'

Lady Morgan slowly turned her head over Mary's shoulder, hissing in what sounded like many tongues – 'It's everyone's fight, Richard, Knight of Galahad. You dare challenge Athena herself?' she questioned.

'That's not a goddess – it is a *child*. And you know it. Release her.' he choked.

'Perhaps you can ask her yourself?' came a gloating reply as Lady Morgan slowly turned Mary to face her accuser. 'Look at this man, my child. You remember, don't you, what he wanted? What they all wanted?' she whispered in her ear. Mary's eyes blazed fiercer; scorn spread across her face.

'*Liars. Murderers.*' came a voice from Mary unlike anything Luke and Richard had heard. The same burning experienced before began to spread all over Richard's skin once more, penetrating deep inside, painful enough to bring him to his knees.

'Mary …' he stuttered. 'Don't do this … don't listen!' came the plea. But Mary's focus grew more and more intense, crushing Richard's ability to speak. With a twitch of her head, he was flung five metres back, landing heavily on his side. Luke's face went pale as he boldly stood his ground, Mary's attention now firmly set on him.

✢　　✢　　✢

Shards of glass flew from the remaining Land Rover, showering down on Iain and Adam. Colonel Thorpe barked orders impatiently.

'How many are there?' Iain asked, crouching lower. Adam poked his head round the rear wheel, only to retract it quickly as a bullet shot past too close for comfort.

'At least half a dozen. Plus, that colonel chap.' he panted. 'We can't deflect that many shots, even between two of us.' he concluded, clenching his fist to summon his shield.

'Can't take that many out with one spear either.' Iain confessed. 'Not spaced out like this.'

Adam quickly surveyed the inside of the vehicle between the volleys for something that could be used to turn the tide their way – stray guns, explosives, anything. Nothing but an empty vodka bottle. He seized it quickly and resumed his defensive position.

'Well, that's empty I'm afraid, lad,' Iain sniggered, despite now perspiring heavily.

'For now,' Adam remarked while he slid under the Land Rover. 'Distraction please,' as he tapped the fuel pipe to fill the bottle. Iain threw a single blue-flamed spear at random over the bonnet, deflected by Colonel Thorpe's own blade. Adam tore off part of his sleeve, stuffing it into the top of the bottle, still ducking from the ricocheting bullets overhead. '*Light.*' he ordered, as Iain brought forth a slight blue flame from his knuckles, enough to light the tip of the rag.

'What's your throwing arm like?' Iain asked.

'Pretty useless,' Adam confessed, while noting how close some guards now were to the vehicle. 'Still ... from this distance? Get ready!' as he brazenly stood and threw the burning bottle neatly at the feet of their advancing attackers, sending up a brief but explosive conflagration. Adam immediately struck the nearest guard on the head with a high kick, Iain tackling another down before landing a solid punch to the jaw. They drew together, Adam presenting his blue shield once more, allowing Iain to toss two more conjured spears towards more distant guards – one making contact in a burst of sparks. A lone bullet deflected from Adam's shield hit Colonel Thorpe in the arm, making him lower his weapon. The moment was enough for Adam to charge towards the remaining guard and land a blunt knee to the chest.

The colonel had swiftly shrugged off his wound and was already hurling his sword towards Iain, who effectively dodged the colonel's brute strength but offered little resistance against a Knight's blade. Adam sprinted and pounced on Thorpe, desperately trying to bring the heavy beast of a man down, arm locked tightly round the throat. Iain took advantage and tried to thrust a spear into his gut, but the sword saw it coming. Options ticking away, Adam clocked the pistol sitting in the colonel's holster and stretched down with a grimace, a finger curling round the grip. He hooked the trigger and squeezed, Thorpe falling to his knees in a squeal of pain as blood soaked through his thigh. Iain ended it with a kick of his own to the forehead as Adam released him.

✣   ✣   ✣

Luke felt that familiar sensation of illness and pain experienced when at Mary's home, this time growing in intensity with every second that passed in her fixated presence.

'You ... know ... me, Min.' he muttered. 'This isn't you. Don't ... become ... what you ... are *not*.'

'You don't know who I am. *What* I am.' Mary cursed. 'What am I to you? You *lied*. You *cheated*. You *hurt* me.' her eyes incandescent.

Luke paused to help cope with the suffering inflicted, took a deep breath. 'You're wrong, Min. I do know you. You are Mary Cassidy. Intelligent, kind, full of compassion. Always there for people.... even when you feel people may have abandoned you. Like I did. This was my fault, I loved you, I still do, and always will – no matter what you believe you are or what you've done or will do. You are Mary Cassidy, and Jenny couldn't have wished for a closer friend.' he wheezed towards the end, holding back stinging tears welling from both emotion and physical agony.

Mary stood silent, her lower lip quivering as she absorbed every word Luke uttered. 'Jenny,' she thought – memories of moments together, laughing and joking. A shoulder to cry on when upset, the times when Jenny's parents had thrown her out and she had nowhere to go. Growing up in the absence of love ... was it any wonder she turned to her for help, and to Luke? The fight within her grew, and with it the fire around her – bolts of fresh lightning lit the skies once more before striking the ground. The surge was enough to break the conflict between Sir Lawrence, William and Karen raging behind, with Gary thrown from his position on top of Tristan, who was up until that point winning the attrition of blades. Adam and Iain ran up to the ruins, spear and shield charged and ready, only to stop short of the tempest Mary was commanding.

Lady Morgan took Mary's arm once more – 'You think you can control this? This power? You can't … it has only one purpose, and you are fulfilling it!' she said, an edge of panic and desperation in her voice for the first time, knowing how close she was to the Palladium – still moving ever closer across the seas. Mary looked at its speck of light in the distance, steadily growing stronger, only to turn back to Luke. No expression, just a pensive gaze as the storm around them tapered off. Luke felt the discomfort ease, enough to stretch a hand out to Mary across the dying circle of fire between them. Mary did not accept it. Instead, she placed both her hands on the wrists of an increasingly flustered Lady Morgan and simply stated – 'I know who I am.'

Mary took a step back, then another – shuffling away from Lady Morgan towards the edge of the cliff top. Lady Morgan reached out in protest, tangled grey hair sweeping across her face, body not able to get closer despite the noticeable effort of trying, Mary appearing to hold her once grey eyes, now a piercing green, at length.

A parting smile to Luke and she fell.

## Chapter 20

Bath, England

1st December 2011 AD.

Nick dragged two stubborn, heavy oak tables from near the fireplace at The Bear to free the regular place in the corner for the tired artificial Christmas tree, Violet busy bending the wire branches into shape while Karen dug around the box of decorations. William sipped a coffee while perched on a bar stool, always more of a traditionalist when it came to festive celebrations – start on Christmas Day and observe the 12 days that follow. He muttered his discontent.

The events of the past week had taken their toll, and while eager to maintain some sort of regularity in seeing out the year, broaching conversation within the group was now laboured in a manner not experienced before. Still, there was a quiet recognition that stood as a reminder that no one person felt blame or grievance towards another. What had happened was now history, what has started was every person's responsibility.

Adam sat quietly alongside Gary as they watched the latest news on *BBC World*. A female reporter, looking like a claymation figurine, stood in Portsmouth harbour concluding a story on how the UK Government was to explore the wreckages of both the German battleship *Bismarck* and, with luck, British battlecruiser *RMS Hood* in honour and celebration of the Battle of the Atlantic seventy years prior. Iain stood leaning against the doorframe, making scoffing noises at the undoubted true purpose of the salvage. Lady Morgan may have been denied possession of the Palladium at Tintagel, but there was no doubt she now knew of its location – and Sir Lawrence and the White Dragon would only need to commit suitable resources under a plausible cover story to obtain it.

While Gary flicked through some research papers about recruits aboard the *Bismarck* during its fateful voyage across the North Sea – referencing the Von Lamorak Family throughout both World Wars, and the likely presence of Michael Von Lamorak through a stained vintage sepia photograph from the 1920s – Adam's thoughts had drifted to his brother, who'd be arriving back at Heathrow anytime now. Upon hearing from neighbours that their mother had been found dead in an apparent breaking and entering job, Luke had dutifully flown out to take care of all the formalities. Combined with this was the burden of having to share Mary's untimely fate with extended family members and friends back in Boston – a task Adam knew would likely incur poisonous wrath against him in the wake of Jenny's death. He cleared his throat before excusing himself and making his way outside for fresh air. Iain took the time to put his hand on his shoulder and give a welcoming smile as he passed him. Adam, grateful for the gesture, forced a smile in return.

A mild evening greeted him outside, the quiet disturbed only by the occasional chatter from students as they passed by the pub entrance enjoying the last week of the season before the holidays. He rubbed his wrists with curiosity. A light blue ring glowed before fading as quickly as it appeared. He had grown in confidence over these past few years, and up until now felt he had nothing to lose other than integrity – but the landscape had shifted, and for the first time those closest to him were at stake, through no fault of their own. This battle, whatever form it was to take, was not going to discriminate or be held purely to their rules anymore. Iain perched beside him – 'Is it always this warm round here this time of year?' he engaged in small talk.

'You'd rather it was snowing? Bath might disappoint.' Adam joked.

'Well, I've never been great at building snowmen … but, it would be good if just for once the places actually resembled the scenes depicted on Christmas cards. Right?' Iain chortled with a stretch and a yawn. 'You know … about your Mam, if you wanted to talk …?' he offered to Adam, sincerely. Adam continued to stare through the buildings opposite before turning to him with a simple 'Thanks.'

Richard's car pulled up; Luke stepped out with a backpack slung over his shoulder. Adam embraced him warmly but didn't burden him with questions about the trip – the look on Luke's face said enough. He passed between the two of them into The

Bear, where the hospitable voices of Karen and Violet could be heard.

'How was it?' Adam asked Richard. His father tilted his head with a shrug and gave muted approval, his mind elsewhere. Iain offered a handshake in condolence, accepted by Richard.

'Did you hear the news? The *Bismarck* salvage?' Iain called out. Richard nodded, they had picked it up on the radio as he and Luke drove back.

'They'll have it by now, won't they? The Palladium.' Adam cautiously proposed. Richard again gave a remorseful nod, recognising that despite Mary's sacrifice, it might have been too late. He raised his hands, placing one on each of Adam's and Iain's arms – 'You two look out for each other, agreed?' looking intensively at both of them. Adam and Iain both nodded and concurred as Richard was beckoned in by William and Gary from the window.

Iain turned to Adam – 'I've got your back, lad, if you've got mine?' Adam gave a blush that was now familiar to Iain and playfully punched Iain's left pectoral – 'Give it a rest will you?' As the two returned inside, Luke was flat out asleep in one of the armchairs, clutching the small photograph of Mary and Jenny tightly, Violet gently tucking a blanket around him. Richard sat in his usual spot with William, Karen, Gary and Nick gathered attentively around him, all voicing opinions. Adam waited until his father beckoned him once more over to the group. He complied. 'Both of you,' Richard insisted, pointing to Iain. The two stood to attention.

'We've been conferring – and our options are limited.' Richard said. 'The White Dragon, we have to assume, have both the Necklace of Harmonia and now the Palladium once more.'

'Which they have had time and time again, Richard.' Nick spoke with grievance on the topic, already suggesting his disapproval of what was coming.

'I know Nick, but this time I fear things may be different. These past few decades have given our enemies much to contemplate, and while their influence has remained resolute, it may now be a time of seismic change – a shift the likes of which none of us have ever seen,' Richard continued with purpose.

'Like what? More world wars? What would be the gain, other than the endless cycles we've experienced before?' William mused, sounding equally sceptical.

'The White Dragon and Lady Morgan have committed unfathomable crimes across the world; yes, that much we know. But this world is changing, we know it, they know it. What if they feel their influence since losing the Palladium has been weakened, tarnished? What better way to remind all beings and loyal followers, to reaffirm Lady Morgan and Sir Lawrence's complete power, that follow up with an event so great in magnitude that every city, country and continent would know?' Richard asked.

'An ultimate war? A true apocalyptic event? Surely not?' Karen shuddered in contemplation. Richard gave a concerned look towards his friends. Glances of fear were exchanged at just the thought of such a reality.

William broke the silence – 'So, what would you have us do?' All turned to Richard aside from Luke, who by this time was snoring. Richard quickly gulped down the last of his beer then cleared his throat.

'Hopefully you'll all now agree. We need to find Mack.'

## The Sacred Band Trinity – Palladium : END

## PART.2 : EXCALIBUR

UK Copyright 2020

Reg. 28473591

Printed in Great Britain
by Amazon